Lokelani Nights

Sharon K. Garner

In memory of my father, Walter Russell Plowman,
my National Geographic travel companion.
He would have loved Lokelani. This one is for you, Dad.

ISBN: 0-7599-4234-X
Trade Paperback
Published February 2006

Ebook ISBN: 1-58200-578-8
Published June 2000

Hard Shell Word Factory
PO Box 161
Amherst Jct. WI 54407
books@hardshell.com
http://www.hardshell.com

Printed in the United States of America

Chapter 1

"TWO WEEKS of work on Lokelani? With your nephew?" Casey Ward echoed her employer's words in a toneless voice. She hadn't lived in Hawaii long but she'd heard of the small, privately owned island.

Patty Kahana, a tiny woman with upswept salt and pepper hair and an hourglass figure, looked uneasy for just a moment. "Perhaps longer. All quite innocent and above board, I assure you. It's highly unusual, I know, but Christopher is a reliable family member who needs some rather unusual help right now. I've had a chance to study you these four months you've worked for me, Casey, and I think you're just the kind of woman Christopher described to me for this assignment."

And the only one you dare ask, I'll bet, she thought to herself. "And what kind was that?" she asked sweetly, her curiosity barely overcoming her anger at the man who had ordered up a woman, not an office temp.

"Attractive, sedate, level-headed, and not fanciful." A reassuring smile was tacked onto the words.

Casey thought about that for a moment. Should she at last tell Mrs. Kahana that she felt someone else had been living inside her skin since she moved to Hawaii four months ago? And that she was the least sedate person known to her friends on the mainland? Or that she was up for a good fairy tale or ghost story anytime? Or that being betrayed by her LAPD lieutenant fiancé, then physically assaulted by him, had made her lose the laughter in her life and she was desperate to find it again?

She looked at Mrs. Kahana's kind, hopeful face. Bad idea right now. "If these aren't executive secretarial duties, just what would I be doing?" she asked instead.

Patty Kahana got up and came around the desk. She always wore a *holoku*, the long, fitted Hawaiian dress but without the train, and a white hibiscus in her hair. Despite her small stature she managed to look regal.

Casey nearly fell out of her chair when the dignified woman hopped up onto the corner of her executive desk to sit. Confidence time, Casey silently warned herself. Oh heavens, what was wrong with this guy and did her boss expect her to fix it?

Mrs. Kahana sat on her precarious perch with her back ramrod straight. "Christopher took a leave of absence from the Honolulu Police Department after he was wounded for the second time in the line of duty. While he decides what he wants to do, he has agreed to quietly look into some incidents on the island for a family friend who owns most of it. Christopher thinks it's best if he blends in as a guest staying at Lokelani Farms. So, he asked me to find someone to pose as the other half of a troubled couple. Separate accommodations, of course. You'll be his 'cover' for snooping around the island. He assures me there's no danger involved or I would have refused our services." She looked at Casey expectantly.

Casey groaned inwardly. Just what she needed right now, a hot shot who'd been shot and was still hanging off the edge of law enforcement. After what Luke had put her through, it would serve this one right if she went disguised as a snag-toothed hag who called it a May/December marriage.

When Casey opened her mouth to refuse, Mrs. Kahana quietly added, "If you decide to accompany him, you'll be paid Kahana Temps' highest rate, plus a bonus because of the unorthodox nature of this assignment. And you'll have my deepest appreciation for helping me out in a difficult situation. You've already demonstrated your discretion and tact, Casey. Christopher and I will depend on your practicing both on this assignment."

'This assignment, should you choose to accept it...' Mission Improbable, Casey thought to herself. At least this job was different, and she needed a change. Again. Maybe this new place and new experiences would shake loose the nothingness inside her. Better to come back to life all over the boss's nephew than the boss.

"I'll take it, thank you, Mrs. Kahana," she said meekly.

Patty Kahana let out a sigh of relief that ruffled Casey's blonde hair. "Thank you, Casey," she said as she hopped off the desk and returned to the high-back leather chair behind it, all business again.

"Lokelani Farms is a working ranch and macadamia nut farm that takes a few paying guests at a time. The guests may help out in the grove, I understand, so you'll need mostly casual clothes and a few work clothes, as well as several evening outfits. They're not formal but they do change for dinner. Some sturdy boots wouldn't come amiss for riding and hiking. Christopher will pick you up at eight o'clock tomorrow morning at your apartment."

She had Casey's sharp, unwavering attention when she hesitated then spoke as if she had come to a decision. "Life has dealt my nephew some severe blows, but he continues to be a nice man. He'll take good care of you."

A PERSISTENT, heavy pounding on her apartment door the next morning dragged her up from the depths of dreamless sleep. She'd finally managed a few hours' rest near dawn. The ruffled elastic band she'd worn to bed had come out of her hair in the night, and she finger-combed the full, wavy, shoulder-blade length stuff out of her eyes as she tumbled out of bed. One glance at the clock told her she'd overslept. It was probably Christopher Kahana trying to break down her door.

Opening the door as far as the heavy-duty security chain permitted, she was immediately impaled by eyes the color of the Hawaiian sky. Their huge owner wore white cotton slacks and a muted aloha shirt in pale blues. With one big hand, he removed his wide-brimmed straw hat with its tapa cloth band, freeing a shock of thick, shining brown hair so dark that it was almost black.

While she gathered her thoughts and her excuses together, she waited for him to speak. Instead, he studied her face, eyes, and hair with quiet intensity. Gee, maybe he didn't like white-gold blondes who—

Oh heavens, she probably *did* look like a snag-toothed hag this morning. Her eyes, no doubt, resembled two blue-green marbles dropped into a can of spaghetti. There went her one chance to make a really good first impression. She studied him back and liked what she saw. He reminded her of someone she couldn't place.

He stared at her a moment longer then shook his head, as if to clear it. "Casey Ward," he finally said, accusing tones in his deep, soft voice. "I'm Christopher Kahana and it's eight o'clock." He consulted the watch on his wrist, a timepiece that looked complicated enough to run a small city.

She blinked and mentally snapped her fingers when she caught the resemblance that had eluded her. Christopher Kahana was a Hawaiian tiki god come to life.

His broad forehead, high cheek bones, and wide, expressive mouth might have been carved from warm, light brown *hapa* wood. He certainly wore the glower of a *hapa* wood tiki. However, a redeeming hint of dimples showed in each cheek, and this angry tiki was big, well-muscled all over, and tall with it, at least six feet four inches.

When she didn't answer him immediately, he inquired in an insulting tone, "You do speak?"

Casey shook herself out of her tiki fantasy and nodded. "Frequently. And I can tell time, too. But I can't sing a note," she explained, her voice soft with sleep. "I was up late packing and I must have gone back to sleep. I'm sorry."

Her old oversize LAPD T-shirt covered her to mid-thigh, but it wasn't nearly enough for the disturbing eyes of this stranger who was suddenly doing some looking. She pulled farther back, until nothing but her face showed, sideways, around the edge of the door. She felt her hair swing free. The tiki god's wide-set eyes followed its swaying mass.

Now, when he didn't answer her, she jumped into the gap. "I apologize, Mr. Kahana. I'll meet you in the lobby in fifteen minutes," she said hurriedly and tried to close the door.

He deftly slid one large white running shoe into the gap, and his soft-timbered, deep voice took on the patient tone of a keeper. "Open the door. I can brief you while you get ready."

He was using cop talk already. What a great start to this day, she thought to herself as her gaze skipped from his face to his foot. "Okay. If you'll remove your size twelve, I'll remove the chain. That's how this works." She mimicked his long-suffering tone perfectly. Then she added in a no-nonsense voice. "But first I want to see some ID, please."

His stormy look deepened, his mouth a thin line as he flipped open an ID wallet, sans badge. "By the way, it's a fourteen," he said and slid his foot out of the gap.

She bit her lip in frustration as she closed the door to undo the chain. By now he must have some opinion of her, his aunt's hand-picked choice for her own nephew's assignment. And now she'd smart-mouthed the man to boot.

She got her face in order and opened the door wide. "Come in. I'm really sorry, Mr. Kahana. The late Casey Ward, that's me."

Suddenly conscious of her tanned bare legs and of his eyes on them, she backed away when he took two steps inside and closed the door behind him. He filled to overflowing the width and height of her tiny hall. She scuttled into the bedroom and left that door half open, since she would be out of his line of vision, so he could 'brief' her.

His growl followed her. "Yeah, and you just might be the 'left' Casey Ward."

She froze. How did he know? she wondered for one wild, brief moment. Was 'Luke Trace reject' stamped on her forehead? When she finally understood his meaning, she mentally shook herself and got on with what she had to do, at warp speed.

He didn't waste any time. She recognized the tone and lack of inflection in the words. It was cop talk again. Luke used to sound the same way when he filled her in on the few cases he decided to tell her about.

"Paul Malo is the controlling partner in the Lokelani Farms operation, a macadamia nut farm and cattle ranch on a small island off the coast of Kauai," he began. "Some weird stuff has been happening and he wants me to quietly check it out." By the fading then strengthening of his voice, she visualized him pacing around her small living room.

She paused to listen to his deep, soft tones. She loved his voice, like being beat about the ears with great big feathers. When she caught herself standing still, she rushed through the rest of her morning routine. Lipstick and blusher would have to do. She simply tossed all her cosmetics, lotions, and scents into her overnight case.

The T-shirt went into the clothes hamper. She would cut it up for dust cloths when she got back. She stuffed a white sleep shirt with a gecko on the front into her case.

"How weird?" she asked cautiously as she pulled on the white cotton slacks she'd laid out the night before, after she'd showered and washed her hair.

He didn't answer immediately and when he did his words were muffled as though he was turned away from her and bending over. The family pictures on the end table, she guessed. Luke was not among them.

"Simple stuff at first. His partner, Kimo White, was swimming off their beach when his clothes disappeared from the beach shack. The same for the girl who works in the house and a young male guest who was with her. Then someone broke the tools that the workers use in the grove, and the saddle girths on three saddles were cut. Their foreman and ranch hands had falls. Luckily, they weren't hurt." He was standing upright now and he was close to her door. She glanced at the opening in alarm.

She hurriedly shrugged on a Hawaiian print turquoise silk shirt, and slid her feet into matching espadrilles. “You’re saying the pranks are escalating?”

“And then some. Paul called me this morning from Ohelo, the little town on the other side of the island. That’s where the only phone is located. Cell phones won’t work in the valley. Last night someone slashed the tires on the Jeep they use to get around the island.”

She was tying her hair back from her face with a narrow turquoise scarf as she walked into the living room. “Does Paul Malo have any idea why this is happening?”

Christopher Kahana, after a quick but thorough inspection of her, effortlessly picked up her heavy suitcases that stood ready beside the front door. “He’s too close. He’s hoping the who will tell him the why. I’m willing to look at it from either direction.”

Casey saw warm approval in his startling eyes as his gaze skimmed over her again. She felt her face grow warm in response. When they reached the street, she was equally aware of the sidelong glances he received from passing women, tourists and residents alike.

She couldn’t believe it when he stopped beside a beat-up old station wagon. She walked from the back end to the hood examining the peeling paint. “Is it contagious?” she asked then grinned.

“I left my good car at home. She’ll get us where we’re going.” He patted a fender. It moved.

Casey climbed in while he put her suitcases in the back with his. She watched in fascination as the door on the driver’s side opened and a large foot and one long, hard-muscled leg joined her, followed by the rest of him. For a big man he moved with an economy of motion.

The car was clean inside and the powerful engine was fine-tuned so that it thrummed when he turned the switch. He smoothly slid them into the stream of traffic.

“We’re going to be late anyway, so how about some breakfast? I’ll join you.” He looked at her and, finally, smiled.

Casey blinked at the now-smiling tiki god. His white teeth and sky-blue eyes almost glowed against the contrast of his tawny skin. And, boy, did he have dimples. Mega. A girl could lose herself in them they were so deep. Suddenly, in an intuitive flash, she knew exactly what he had looked like when he was eight years old, and now, that dimpled smile was an open invitation to join him in this adventure.

“Kona coffee, please,” she managed in a voice that was almost normal.

Deep inside her something snapped, then opened wide. She felt the laughter of a child and her own love of life quietly pour into the void when she took a deep, cleansing breath. She'd given the faithless cop on the mainland all the head time he deserved, and then some. It was time to move on. She embraced her journey back to life, which was beginning now. At any moment her powerful emotions might do a decent imitation of a volcano and erupt right there on the seat beside this handsome cop.

She realized that Christopher Kahana didn't have a clue about what was happening to her as he drove them through the sun-filled, morning-fresh streets of Honolulu to a shopping center. In an open courtyard cafe ringed with palm trees and other tropical plants, he ordered two breakfasts of macadamia nut muffins with sweet butter and a pot of Kona coffee.

She'd fallen in love with Kona coffee the moment she first tasted it. When their pudgy, red-haired waitress brought their meal, she immediately poured out two cups of the dark, steaming brew, sweetening and lightening hers.

Closing her eyes, she took three tiny sips, savoring each before swallowing. After the third sip she gave a little shiver of delight at its sweet richness. When she opened her eyes, Christopher Kahana was watching her closely, his beautiful lips slightly parted.

She put down her cup while she looked back. "So, we're a couple trying to stay together. What's our problem?" One of the warm, tender muffins split apart with just the lightest pressure from her fingers.

He gaze had dropped to watch her hands at their work and he looked up in surprise. He shrugged. "I don't know. You're just cover, a reason for being there, and in separate rooms. The pretense of spending time together will give me a chance to go everywhere, do everything, see everything. Paul wants to keep it low key until he finds out who's doing this and why."

Thoughtfully, she buttered a piece of her muffin. "I refuse to be unfaithful. *You* were unfaithful. You're an absolute hound when it comes to women. I really don't know why I ever married you."

He gaped at her, a stunned expression on his handsome features. She watched him gather his wits and leap to his own defense. "I am not a hound when it comes to women," he declared in injured tones.

"We have separate rooms. We took off our wedding rings. It looks bad." She gazed past him to their red-haired waitress with the overbite who stood frozen beside his chair, their bill clutched in her right hand. "And it's all because you can't keep your hands off redheads. They're your weakness, and I refuse to dye my hair red or wear a red wig when we make love. That's what set you off this time, Kit."

The waitress twitched and the movement drew his attention. He muttered a rude word under his breath when he found the woman, agog, beside his elbow. He quickly informed her they didn't need anything else and grabbed the bill out of her hand. She reluctantly left them, casting wary glances over her shoulder.

He sent Casey a quelling look. "That was not funny. And my name is Christopher," he hissed at her across the table.

She allowed herself a devilish grin while she gave him a considering stare. "Too long."

He looked alarmed. "Chris, then."

"Too ordinary. Kit suits you. Besides, Kit and Casey Kahana has a nice ring to it." She looked at him brightly over the rim of her cup as she sipped more of the delicious Kona brew.

His eyes narrowed suspiciously. "You're not going to be a problem, are you?"

She was a picture of wide-eyed innocence. "Me? I just like my ducks in a row, especially now when you'll be lying through your teeth and I'm along for the ride. That's not unreasonable, is it?" She smiled at him as if he really was eight years old and she was his patient partner in crime.

Frowning, he reached up and tugged on his left earlobe while he stared into his cup, as if the answer to what he was getting himself into might be written there. She noticed his cup was half empty, so she refilled it from the pot.

Apparently, he decided to take her reasoning at face value, her odd behavior as a temporary aberration. "You're right about the rings. We'd better stop and buy a set."

"Size six. Tell me about yourself." When he didn't answer immediately, she quickly added, "No big, dark secrets. Just everyday stuff. We're not joined at the hip, you know. What if we're apart and someone asks questions? I see you take your coffee as it comes."

When he decided to speak, the words were again in expressionless cop talk. He could have been reading off his grocery list to her. "My name is Christopher Allan Kahana. I'm twenty-nine years old. I was born on Kauai. My parents still live there, both teachers. I have three brothers and two sisters spread out all over the Islands. Besides Uncle Allan, who's married to your boss Patty, I have an Uncle Matt on Hawaii, the Big Island. He has a ranch there. I was with the HPD six years. I was wounded two separate times in the line of duty and I've taken a leave of absence to decide whether I still want to be a cop. Not married, present company excepted, but I thought about it once." There was a little hiccup in his voice just there. "Favorite color, blue. I'll eat almost anything except squid. I don't smoke. I drink a little. I swear a little more. I sleep in my underwear. I boogie board, surf, and hike in my spare time."

When his voice stopped, he slowly leaned toward her, something in his eyes making her lean back. "If I tell you about me, you'll tell me about you. That's how this works," he finished quietly.

She felt her eyes open wide. Oh, he was good, throwing back her own words from earlier. This looked more and more like fun, she thought to herself, pausing to wonder where 'wounded in the line of duty' was located exactly on that long, firm, sturdy body.

A slow smile began as she leaned forward, her eyes boring into his across twelve inches of Hawaiian air. Now it was his turn to lean back one inch at a time.

She adopted his tone of voice precisely, or Luke's, she wasn't sure which. Kit Kahana was in her sights but Luke Trace was in her mind.

"As you can see, I take my coffee light and sweet. My name is Casey Anne Ward. I'm twenty-six years old. I was born in San Diego, raised mostly in Washington state, a Navy brat. Parents dead. They hitched a ride on the wrong Navy transport plane. One brother, a computer systems analyst in Seattle. I moved to LA when I was 21, moved to Hawaii four months ago. Never married but I came close." Her voice ground to halt and she swallowed, despite her determination not to acknowledge the memory. His eyes narrowed but he didn't comment.

She cleared her throat and continued. "I'm an executive secretary. A good one. I don't smoke. I don't drink. I swear mildly. Favorite color, turquoise, because it makes my eyes, which are blue-green, look turquoise. I've sworn off men temporarily and peanut butter permanently, ask me when we know each other better." That was another memory that stopped her cold. She was aware that his eyes wouldn't miss the color warming her cheeks.

"You know what I sleep in. All those things you do in your spare time sound physically painful. When I'm not working, I read, volunteer at a shelter for battered women, and I swim and walk a lot."

His eyes snagged hers, a question and a warning in them. "My aunt thinks very highly of you," he said softly.

She met his gaze with all the honesty and sincerity she could muster. "Point taken, Mr. Kahana. I like her, too. A lot. And I owe her a lot. I came here with just my clothes and no job prospects. Hers was the first temp agency I tried because I liked the way Kahana looked in the telephone book—and it was a name I could pronounce. Patty administered proficiency tests on the spot, hired me, and got me my apartment. And she didn't ask any questions about why I was here with just my clothes and no job prospects." Her mind skittered around the reason it took her only two weeks to leave her old life and come to Hawaii.

"She put me to work right away and it's been steady for four months. When I do a job, I give it my best shot. And I'm loyal. I think she knows that by now."

He nodded, still holding the check in his hand. "Come on, Ms. Kahana. Time to fly."

He paused when she said, "I prefer Mrs. Kahana, if you don't mind."

Window shopping in Honolulu was her only real vice. They started out side-by-side to walk to a jewelry store in the shopping center. Soon he was in the lead when her steps slowed so she could admire the many goods on offer. When he found himself walking alone, he strode back to where she stood goggle-eyed beside a display window, took her hand, and pulled her away. And he didn't let go until they reached the jewelry store.

He stopped outside and dropped her hand. "No funny stuff in here, or so help me, I'll do something you'll regret."

"Promises, promises," she muttered. At his threatening look she said meekly, "Whatever you say, dear," and slid her hand back into his because it felt like it belonged there.

"And stop scowling like that," she whispered. "This is supposed to be a happy time. If I have to behave, you have to behave."

She pulled him inside then froze. A luscious redhead stood behind the counter, waiting to help them. Casey was aware of Kit's gaze swiveling in her direction, but it was the intense, bordering on painful, pressure on her fingers enclosed in his that made her swallow her giggle and any reckless words that might follow on its heels.

He stepped up to the counter with her in tow. "We'd like to buy a set of wedding bands, please. Lower end of the price range. Sizes six and thirteen."

One of the woman's arched brows rose into her forehead and she looked at Casey with pity in her eyes. Casey clamped her jaws together in frustration. Now that she was closer, Casey saw that the woman was pregnant and just starting to show beneath the attractive maternity dress she wore.

"Maybe rings in sterling silver rather than platinum or white gold?" Casey suggested.

She felt Kit's body tense beside her. He let go of her hand and casually circled her waist with his arm, pinching her lightly on her side.

She flinched. "We're pinching pennies. On a tight budget," she said quickly when she felt his fingers move again, at the ready.

"I understand perfectly," the woman said, smiling and pulling a tray of silver band rings out of the display case in front of them. "Broad or narrow?"

Casey looked up at Kit, letting the decision be his.

"Narrow."

In no time they had tried on the sterling silver rings, the woman rang up the sale, and Kit paid the bill.

The woman handed Kit the fancy little tissue bag with the ring boxes inside. "There you are, sir. Priced right for tight budgets."

Casey couldn't resist when she heard the woman's inflection and saw her false smile. "Thank you for your help." She placed both hands over her flat stomach. "I'm sure you understand how it is when there's a baby on the way."

She saw Kit's jaw go slack, so she threaded her arm through his and hurried him outside, the woman's hasty congratulations floating along behind them.

"I'm sorry, Kit." She pulled him along beside her toward the lower level and the parking lot, where he could kill her in private. "I almost made it."

He was making noises like a tea kettle coming to a boil. "Almost doesn't count!"

"Well, she thought you were being cheap, not thrifty, so-so I gave her a reason she identified with," she finished lamely.

He pulled her into a niche with a bench that was tucked between two stores, then swung her around to face him. "Now listen to me, Casey Anne Ward. You *will* play it straight on Lokelani. Or I'll—I'll—tell my Aunt Patty."

She crossed her arms over her chest, laughter bubbling up. "Oh, yeah? Well, I'll tell my big brother and he'll come over here and beat you up."

His dismayed stare held her eyes. "I knew it. You're crazy and my aunt doesn't know."

Her smile vanished. Time to get serious and soothe his fears. "No,

I'm not crazy, Kit. It's just...well, I haven't had much to laugh about for the past six months. And there's something about you or this assignment, maybe a combination of both, that brings out the devil in me. Anyway, I apologize if I embarrassed you."

He let out his breath. "This isn't a game. You do understand that? If you can't handle it, I want to know right now."

She shook her head and caught her lower lip between her teeth. His intent stare moved to her mouth. "I'll behave and I'll play my part well. I promise to be an asset rather than a liability to you, boss."

He looked worried again. "Don't go too far the other way, now. Be yourself, but with—restraint. Okay?"

She nodded and smiled gently. "Restraint in place, dear."

Casey, subdued for the moment, sat quietly at his side as he drove them around Diamond Head and through affluent residential districts to a small airstrip.

A mechanic in greasy, cut-off bib overalls waved to them, and a uniformed cop sat in an unmarked car. He got out and came over to them when they got out of the station wagon. She saw the long, curious look he sent her way.

Kit briefly introduced her to Officer Dan Hatala and Moki. He explained that Moki kept his plane and the station wagon in running order.

On his introduction Moki gave her that startling big Hawaiian grin. "Hey, Koa, she's ready to fly," he said to Kit and gestured toward a plane sitting poised at the end of the short runway. Then he ambled away.

"What's going on, Dan?" Kit finally asked the officer.

"Security is tight on all outgoing flights, especially from small airstrips like this. You hear on the grapevine about the big robbery two days ago?" he asked Kit.

Kit shook his head. "I've been off-island, Kauai way, visiting my folks. Just got back. What went down this time?"

"A priceless collection of carved jade figurines being transported in an armored car from a bank vault to a museum for a limited showing. We're keeping a lid on this one for as long as we can."

"This makes the fourth major art theft in the city in two years, doesn't it?" Kit asked.

Dan nodded. "Sorry, Chris, I'll have to check your bags and the plane. Where you headed?"

Kit talked, but gave very little information, while he unloaded everything from the station wagon onto the ground. Casey opened her suitcases for the officer. She was surprised at how thoroughly he went through everything. Moki helped Kit unload the things that were already in the plane. Officer Dan did the same with those items then checked the plane itself. She noticed that the pile of cargo included four new tires for Lokelani's Jeep.

The only objects that got any reaction or comment were the rings. Officer Dan raised his eyebrows when he opened the boxes in the jewelry store bag and saw the matching bands.

"Don't ask," Kit said quickly, looking uncomfortable. "I'm on a private job."

The cop looked aside at Casey. "Yeah, tough work for guys on leave." He did a double take when she closed one twinkling eye in a broad wink.

Kit saw it and she waited tensely for his reaction. Had she gone too far? Was her idea of 'restraint' too loose for his tastes? He simply shook his head in silent surrender while the corners of his mouth lifted upward, then he changed the subject.

With a little smile to herself, she closed her suitcases and the three men loaded them and the tires into the cargo hold of the red and white plane. When they finally taxied away, she returned Dan's and Moki's shaka signs and was rewarded with two big grins.

She had quickly learned that the shaka was a side-stretched little finger and jutting thumb, with the three fingers in between folded against the palm. Presented with a twisting motion of the wrist, it meant 'hang loose' in the special language of Hawaii.

The lingering smile slid off her face when she realized they had lifted off. She gasped while Kit spoke briefly into the radio.

"Are you all right?" His eyes remained straight ahead.

She was ashamed of her tiny, breathless voice. "First time in a small plane. White knuckles and sweaty palms."

He glanced at her then. "It's safer than a car. If you're going to be sick, there's a bag in the pocket on the side of your seat."

"I didn't move to Hawaii to throw up," she came back at him. "I might enjoy the ride. Eventually."

Fifteen minutes later she released the sides of the seat from her strangle hold on them and wanted to talk. "Why did Moki call you Koa?"

He smiled and she got half volume on the dimple in his right cheek. It was a shame to waste them on the windshield like that, she decided.

"I sometimes get the nickname because of my build. There's a tree called a *koa*."

Nodding in agreement, her gaze slid down over him, taking inventory of his long, powerful limbs, wide shoulders, and hard-muscled body.

He continued. "It also means brave and fearless. A lot of Hawaiian words have two meanings."

"And Lokelani, what does that mean? Sometimes I have trouble pronouncing Hawaiian words," she confided. "Your aunt gave me a book to study. It helped."

"The *loke lani* is a small red rose, but the words taken separately can also mean heavenly rose. That's how I think of Lokelani. It's kind of shaped like two roses close together. Remember there are only thirteen letters in the Hawaiian alphabet, and you usually pronounce each letter in a word."

"Easy for you to say, Hawaiian born and bred. Oh, before we forget." She dug in the jewelry store bag for the ring boxes. She opened hers and slid the ring on. "Left hand, please." He let go of the yoke with his left hand and held it across his body. "With this ring, I give thee cover," she said and slipped it onto his ring finger.

"Let's hope we blend in," he answered.

She put the ring boxes inside the bag and stuffed it into the pocket on the side of her seat. "You know, there are still things we need to discuss, things we should know about each other if we're married."

"For instance?"

She almost laughed at his cautious tone. "Well, unless you admit to being a cop, you'll need an occupation. It has to be high income or we couldn't afford to come here or rent or fly this plane."

He was quiet for a second. "The trip is a present from rich parents. The plane is theirs."

She nodded. "Okay, a patch job by the in-laws, your side. You'll still need a career. I can stick with mine. The less we invent, the better. How about owner of Kahana Temps, making plans to open branches on the other islands, maybe on the mainland? You can clear it with your aunt."

"Sold."

They used the rest of their air time to go over their stories, including details. For simplicity's sake, they decided to use her four months in Hawaii as the length of their brief and shaky marriage. Supposedly, Kit had met and married her in LA. They shared everything from where they had gone to school, to siblings' names, to their tastes in music.

"Kauai, dead ahead," he said shortly after they fell into a companionable silence. "Have you visited the other islands yet?"

"No, I haven't been off Oahu." Her voice sounded wistful to her own ears. "I can't afford it."

She was surprised at his response. "Well, the next time I fly home or to one of the other islands, I'll give you a call first. You can come along for the ride. I'm sure I have a relative or two or six, plus my parents, who would be happy to have you stay with them."

"That would be great. Thank you," was all that came into her mind to say.

They flew along a shoreline where lacy white waves gathered around the bases of green vertically pleated cliffs and edged golden, sandy beaches.

"The cliffs are called the *pali*." She heard the love for his home island echo in his words. "Some of those valleys are so steep and narrow that only one person can stand in them, if they can get to them. *Uluhe* fern is all that grows on them."

Casey gazed, entranced, at the undulating folds with their green velvety covering. She twisted in her seat and leaned closer to Kit to look out the window on his side. "It's so beautiful, I could weep," she whispered.

At her quiet words, he suddenly turned his head in her direction. They were almost nose to nose.

She gasped and jerked back, surprised at the jab of fear she felt. She hadn't been that close to a man in four and a half months, and she wasn't in a hurry to change that. She saw the question in his eyes.

"Sorry," she muttered from her seat, unable to offer more.

Kit eventually banked the plane away from the island and Casey held onto her seat again, despite the fact that she hadn't unfastened her seat belt.

"That's Lokelani up ahead in the haze."

It was farther away than it looked. As they slowly drew near, Casey drank in the beauty of the little island, a miniature version of the green-cliffed Kauai, but with lusher growth on the cliffs.

"The *pali* is all that's left of the cones of two small volcanoes that formed the island. They more or less surround the island and cut right through the middle. Lokelani Farms is on the other side of the island, in the crater of one of them. The little town of Ohelo is on this side, in the other crater," he explained to her.

She cleared her throat then spoke. "These volcanoes are extinct, right?" she asked carefully.

Kit laughed, a sound that startled her in a nice way, a sound as rich as her morning coffee, a sound he should make more often.

"So far, so good. They've been quiet for time out of mind."

Casey scarcely heard because she had looked away from him to stare ahead. They passed over Ohelo and were flying straight at the *pali* on Lokelani. Although they cleared it with a couple hundred feet or so to spare, her stomach remained fluttering on the ground floor.

"Oh my," she heard herself say faintly, when she saw what was on the other side.

Roads of rich red earth outlined open grassy areas and circled a grove of dark-leafed trees on the crater's patchwork quilt floor. A wide curve of white sand and a line of trees were the only objects that separated the oblong, bowl-shaped valley floor from the vast Pacific Ocean.

They circled the valley, passing a long, low house just as the plane's engine began coughing and cutting out with frightening regularity. Frowning, Kit fiddled with something on the instrument panel in front of him.

Casey watched, feeling the blood drain from her face as she gripped the edges of her seat, her parents' deaths in a plane crash slashing through her mind.

After a short, steep banking turn, Kit settled the plane lightly on Lokelani Farms' earthen runway.

"I'll have to check that out," he said calmly, apparently unaware of the fear and memories that still held her breath in a painful grip as they taxied to a halt. "I hear there's a great lunch buffet for new guests. Macadamia nut cake for me. What will you have?" He cut the belatedly smooth-running engine.

"An ulcer, I think," she croaked weakly. He stared at her, deadpan, until she added, "And two slices of cake, please."

Laughter danced through his eyes but never made it to his beautiful mouth where her wide-eyed stare ran aground. Against her will, her eyes took a bumpy ride across the chiseled peaks of his upper lip and finally came to rest on the fullness of his lower one.

A pickup truck pulled up beside the plane. With his eyes still on her, Kit made scrabbling sounds on the door panel with his left hand as he searched for the handle. Finally, he slowly turned away and climbed out. Casey, unfolding herself from her painfully tense position, eased open her door.

A small, slim man wearing jeans, a denim shirt, and a disreputable looking straw cowboy hat, ran to help her down. He grabbed his hat off his head when she finally stood on solid ground. His hair was ginger-snap brown with flecks of gray, and his eyes were warm mahogany. He didn't resemble her idea of a rich man, which he surely must be to own most of a Hawaiian island.

"I'm Paul Malo. Welcome to Lokelani Farms," he said, extending his hand to Casey.

His handshake with Kit included a vigorous thump on Kit's right shoulder. Casey saw him wince. The discomfort disappeared in a smile when he answered Paul's questions about his parents, brothers, and sisters.

Kit introduced her as his associate, aka Mrs. Kit Kahana. Casey darted a quick glance at him when she heard him so easily use the nickname she'd given him. He gave Paul a thumbnail sketch of their cover story, ending by asking Paul to drop heavy hints about their strained marriage to explain their separate rooms, any tension between them, and their wanderings.

"Any more trouble today?" Kit asked, opening the cargo door.

When Paul shook his head, Kit asked him for a complete rundown on the other inhabitants and guests of Lokelani Farms.

Casey offered to help with the luggage. Kit handed her the overnight case she'd packed that morning and told her to wait in the truck. She set her case in the truck bed then leaned against the passenger side door so she was able to hear Paul's voice. If Kit thought she was just a mindless prop on this assignment, well, he'd know the bitter truth shortly.

"There are two guests with us, besides yourselves. Adam Hiroki is a friend of my partner Kimo White. He visits a couple of times a year. He's the owner of Heavenly Chocolates based in California. James Dale owns a chain of travel agencies with his parents. He's trying to convince me to allow him to bring small tours here."

Paul hefted her suitcases as easily as Kit, Casey noted, as he swung one up into the bed of the truck.

"Malama Akoa is my housekeeper and has been with me for twenty years. Saito is my foreman. He's been here for three years. Ilima helps Malama in the house. She's from Ohelo and I've known her family all my life. There are two hands on the place. Harry is the newest, from Ohelo. Been here a year. Lono is from the Big Island and has been with me five years."

The men finished the transfer of luggage and tires into the truckbed while Paul talked, Kit listened, and Casey eavesdropped. When they were finished, Casey climbed into the small truck's cab and slid to the middle of the seat to wait, listening to the quiet around them. It was broken now only by an occasional word, the sounds of the sea and wind, and the cries of sea birds.

Kit climbed in and slid his left arm across the back of the seat behind her. It was close quarters, so Casey hesitantly shifted sideways then reluctantly leaned into the curve of him, allowing more room for Paul to use the gear shift.

It was the first time their bodies touched, although their hands had touched many times. This was different, she noticed in nervous surprise. Very, very different. At five feet eight inches tall she fit against him as though his six-feet-four-inch frame had been molded and shaped just for her. His body felt warm and safe and comforting, yet somehow dangerous, all at the same time.

She forced herself to relax against him. There would be times they would have to touch and she couldn't nervously react every time they did. However, she diligently avoided looking at him after one upward glance showed surprise and a warm awareness in those disturbing blue eyes. For one brief moment, when the truck started to move, she was positive she felt his nose in her hair.

The dirt of the road was as red as the exposed earth she'd seen from the air on the *pali* of Kauai. Long, thick green grass, swaying in the steady wind, grew right up to the edges of the road. Grazing groups of sleek, fat brown cattle broke up the expanse of vegetation in irregular patterns. Paul, talking as they went, drove across a cattle grid that allowed the farm's vehicles to cross over from the 'inside' road, inside the fence, to the 'outside' road, which ran parallel but outside the fence.

"Do the cattle just roam free?" she asked Paul during a pause in his running commentary.

He seemed pleased by her interest. "They do until we round them up to cull the herd. The fence separates the center of the valley from the edge where the house, grove, garden, and beach are. The beach path isn't fenced because it's too narrow and winding for cattle to walk. There are a couple of stiles in the fence, like in England, that we can climb over, and gates for access for the *paniolos*, the cowboys, and their horses, and metal cattle grids for the vehicles."

Off to their left, beyond the cattle and grass, Casey saw blue layers of sky and sea. Paul noticed.

"We have one of the loveliest beaches in the Islands. It's wide, clean, and protected by a reef and a breakwater. Stay on the island side of them, though, because there's a wicked undertow just beyond."

Casey wondered why Paul Malo and his partner hadn't sold out to developers by now. She had worked for one through Kahana Temps and she understood how persistent they were. It would be a shame when it happened because Lokelani was as beautiful as it was peaceful.

Soon Paul turned off onto a circular lane lined with palm trees and small, sweet-smelling pink, white, yellow, and red flowering trees. Casey looked at them with pleasure, lifting her face and closing her eyes while she drew a deep breath that was heavy with their strange, exotic scent. When she opened them, Kit was watching her intently. She quickly looked away.

"Plumeria?" she asked Paul.

"Right." Again, Paul seemed delighted with her. "Malama usually wears a lei made from them or has a blossom stuck in her hair."

The dazzling, alternating shadow patterns of solid palm then lacy-leafed plumeria made her senses swim. She caught steadying, tantalizing glimpses of the house through the greenery. At last, it appeared.

A wide, deep verandah protected by a sloping red tile roof provided deep shade for the three visible sides of the one-story house. Behind and soaring above it, like a folding curtain, was the green, sharply fluted *pali*. Paul drove the truck around a planting and parked at the foot of wide wooden steps.

Suddenly, weariness washed over her in a wave. Kit gave her his hand when she stepped out onto the hard brown pieces of material that covered the driveway. The ground beneath the trees was mulched with it also.

Then, a movement in the shadows of the verandah caught her eye. She turned toward it before an eerie stillness settled over everything around her. Even the steady wind from the sea ceased its restless motion.

It was a woman, her brightly patterned red *muumuu* standing out from the shade as she glided to the center of the verandah. She stood six feet tall in her bare feet, because she wore no shoes, and she weighed at least three hundred pounds. Yet she floated forward as if she defied any force that bound her to the earth.

Casey felt herself moving toward the woman, up the steps, yet she wasn't aware of giving her feet orders to climb them.

A creamy white and yellow plumeria blossom broke the coarse darkness of the woman's hair and complimented the light brown shade of her skin. Over her right arm she carried two leis made from pink plumerias.

Casey's gaze moved from the wide, mobile mouth curved in a peaceful smile, past the broad nose, to the shining dark eyes. Like a Hawaiian deity, Malama, for this was surely who it must be, opened her arms and Casey's feet took her forward into them. It was an unnerving experience.

"Welcome to Lokelani," the woman said in a low-pitched, soft voice that rumbled beneath Casey's cheek. She held Casey away from her, slipped a lei over her head, and kissed her on both cheeks. "I am Malama. Aloha, *keiki.* That means child," she whispered and looked Casey up and down until she squirmed. "You eat some food then you sleep."

Casey blinked in surprise then nodded in agreement. "Thank you, Malama, for making me feel so welcome on Lokelani."

Three men came out of the house and lined up beside but a little astern of Malama. Casey felt Kit's presence near her and, feeling shy, she was thankful he was there. He had gotten the lei treatment from Malama and was moving down the reception line, too.

"This is Kimo White, my partner," Paul said, introducing her to a silver-haired man with nut-brown skin.

Kimo White looked nervous and twitchy. He had bags under both eyes, and he wore a soft leather pouch of the same color around his neck on a thin leather strip. He was smoking a pipe full of sweet tobacco. His hand shook when he took the pipe out of his mouth to greet them and shake hands.

"And this is Adam Hiroki," Paul went on. "He owns Heavenly Chocolates in California."

Casey gave him her hand. "I'm familiar with your products, Mr. Hiroki. My mom was crazy about your Dream Creams and rationed them out to us. Now I buy a whole box just for myself."

Mr. Hiroki's mouth spasmed in a quick smile and he shook her hand with a firm grip. He was short and chubby with sleek black hair and a tiny mustache, more of a shadow, on his upper lip. She wondered if that was his best attempt or if he really wanted it to look like that.

He was casually dressed in white from head to toe so that he almost glowed. And he wore a cologne, Oriental and thick, that went right to her sinuses and made them close ranks in protest. Her head pounded at first sniff.

But it was his eyes that held her in thrall. They were black and dead, cold and impenetrable, resembling a stretch of water after an oil spill.

The third man waited for her with his hands thrust deep into the pockets of his stylishly baggy pants and with a cocky grin on his face. He wasn't as tall as Kit, a good six feet to Kit's six feet four, but slim and sandy haired, and altogether too handsome for his own good. His light blue eyes reminded her forcibly of her rogue ex-fiancé.

When Paul introduced Casey to James Dale, the younger man raised her hand to his lips, watching for her reaction, rather than Kit's, as he did so. She knew he was trouble when he held both the hand and the kiss too long. Here was a true hound when it came to women. Luke Trace and the fictional personality she'd slapped on poor Kit, would look like inexperienced puppies beside this master hound.

She withdrew her hand at the same moment she felt Kit's arm drape possessively around her waist, making her jump. James gave Kit a perfunctory handshake, still smiling confidently—until she heard the bones grit in his hand. A look of surprised pain crossed his even features

Another man, an inch or so shorter than her but muscular, watched her from the foot of the verandah steps. He wore jeans, boots, a plaid shirt and a Stetson. A huge belt buckle glinted in the afternoon sun. In it Casey saw the shape of a squat, ugly tiki god. The man and the tiki were both short on smiles.

Paul acknowledged the man with a smile. "This is Saito, our foreman."

He nodded to both of them and tipped his hat to her. "Welcome to Lokelani Farms," he said, his gleaming dark chocolate eyes watchful, taking in Casey from head to toe in a measured glance. She felt her skin crawl before he turned away to unload the truck.

"Come inside," Malama said, making shooing motions with her hands at the men. "I have a late lunch for everyone then I show you your room. The bathroom is this way."

Skirting the others who were filing inside, Saito disappeared around a corner of the verandah, carrying several of their bags. Casey made a little sign to Malama, who was waiting for her, then hung back to wait for Kit.

Kit and Paul had wandered over to the edge of the verandah where it turned another corner of the house. They were looking at something and discussing it quietly. She walked over to them.

Sitting in the shade of a parking area was an ancient, bright yellow open Jeep with extra seats across the back and a canopy with a neat white fringe around it. It bore a striking resemblance to a lemon with a lid. The jaunty little vehicle was sitting at an odd angle, however. It didn't take her long to see why.

Its tires hung in cleanly cut ribbons on its wheels, like razor-sharp claws or teeth had sliced neatly through the heavy rubber, again and again and again.

James Dale, nasty and with more confidence than brains, needed to be taught a lesson.

Kit noticed James almost leaning against his wife just as Casey reached for her coffee cup to accidentally tip it into the hound's lap. Kit quietly took her left hand and laced his fingers with hers, giving the other man a steely look. Almost immediately Casey's fingers thumped from circulation deprivation. Another time, she quietly promised herself. Besides, it would have been a waste of good Kona coffee.

Soon after they finished, Paul invited them into his office to check in. When he included her in the invitation, Casey wondered if he was following their cover, or was just being kind, or if he thought of her as a true working associate of Kit's. It surprised her when she realized how much she wanted to help Kit find out who was violating this beautiful, peaceful place.

As they walked around the *lanai* to the office, Paul described the layout of the house. "The parlor and dining room are across the front." Casey had noticed early on that the Hawaiians call the living room the parlor. "The kitchen, office, my room, and Malama's and Ilima's bedrooms are all along this wing. Kimo's room and the guest bedrooms are on the other side, with yours. All the rooms have doors onto the verandah and the *lanai* for ventilation. There's a large separate guest cottage near the beach. Adam is staying in it."

Both the men were all business once they got inside the privacy of the office. Paul sat down behind the desk and she and Kit took the chairs in front of it.

"You know most of what I'm about to say, Kit, but Casey hasn't heard it," Paul began without preamble.

"I'd like to hear it again. Go ahead," Kit urged.

"It started about a month ago. Someone stole Kimo's clothes while he was swimming. Shortly after James arrived last week, the same thing happened to him and Ilima."

"Have the clothes turned up?" Kit asked.

He shook his head. "A couple of weeks back someone broke the rakes and wheelbarrows we use in the grove every day. I put a lock on the shed where the tools are kept and on the small warehouse in the grove where the nuts are stored for shipment. Malama has the keys."

"They weren't locked before that?" Kit's voice was pure interrogating cop.

"There was no need."

"Then anyone on the farm could have just walked in and done it."

Paul nodded, a sad look on his face. "Or by sea, or by the Ohelo road, or across the *pali*. There's an old trail. We don't have any workers coming over by road from Ohelo or by sea from Kauai to work in the grove at this time of year. It's just us and the guests."

"And the saddle girths?" Casey asked, surprising herself. She didn't bother to look at Kit's expression.

"They were cut nearly through on the underside that goes against the horse's body. On three saddles. When the two hands and Saito rode out, the girths broke. Thank God nobody was hurt. I saved one of the girths to show you. It's in the tool shed in the grove."

She sensed Kit's scowl this time when she asked, "What do Saito and the hands believe is going on?"

Paul looked uncomfortable. "Kit tells me you're new to Hawaii, Casey. We're a superstitious lot. The hands are saying Puhi, a shark god, is angry with us."

"A shark god?" She was thinking along the lines of shredded tires and shark teeth.

"Puhi is our *aumakua*, our family god, and the whole island is *ohana*, family," Paul explained. "He protects those who love Lokelani. His name, in Hawaiian, is about four inches long, so he's known as just Puhi. Malama can tell the story better than I can, but ask her in private. Please."

Kit asked his next question quickly, throwing her a warning look. "What do you think is going on, Paul?"

Paul grinned sheepishly. "I think Puhi is getting bad press, because we've done nothing to incur his wrath. I like to cover all the bases," he said in an aside to Casey. "The real trouble is that this is having a profound effect on Kimo. He's terribly superstitious. He's talking about selling out his share of the farm."

Kit frowned. "That points to the golden boy of travel. I'm sure he'd like to get his hands on any part of Lokelani." Glancing at Casey, he added, "Among other things. He probably has his investors all lined up."

Paul moved in his chair, his feelings showing in his worried frown. "Maybe. But I've saved my biggest worries for last. The safety of our bulls and the turbines that supply our power. Hupo and Pilikia are Lokelani Farms' champion breeding bulls, Casey. They've fathered calves all over the world through artificial insemination. Pilikia means 'trouble' and Hupo means 'not too bright,' and their names suit their personalities. After what happened to the Jeep last night, I'm sleeping in the barn with them. Lono will be spending the nights on the *pali* with the turbines. Would you like to meet the bulls?" he asked, a kid ready to show off a favorite pet.

Kit readily accepted. "I'd like to move my plane to the hangar while we're at it. I need to take a look at it."

Casey declined, opting for unpacking and a nap. Kit handed her over to Malama before he left with Paul. Malama took her to their room, cutting across the courtyard from the office. She went ahead of Casey into the room, flicking on the overhead fan.

Casey looked at the king size bed then scanned the room. Both Kit and his aunt had promised separate accommodations. Then she spied it—a louvered door in the wall beside the bed.

Malama spoke before Casey asked the question. "The connecting door." She glided over and opened it, turning on the fan in that room also.

Saito had put all their cases on the floor inside Casey's verandah doorway. She quickly sorted out Kit's bags and dragged them through the connecting doorway into his room.

Like hers, Kit's room was done in shades of blue with light wood furniture and white draperies, which gave each space an airy feeling. She surreptitiously checked the connecting door. There were locks on both sides.

She caught Malama watching her and purposely left the door wide open. How much did she know? Casey was inclined to tell Malama everything at that moment. Surely the older woman wasn't involved in these pranks. Still, she would have to play by the rules Kit set down until he changed them.

She stammered when she tried to speak and had to start over. "Kit and I are having...problems."

"I know, but you will find each other here, on Lokelani." It was a statement of fact and Malama punctuated it by sitting down on the bed, ready to be mother confessor.

Casey plunged ahead, hoping she sounded more convincing than she felt. "We've only been married four months, you see, and we're having trouble learning to live with each other."

Malama nodded and patted the bed beside her. "The man who hurt you deeply was not Kit, I think. But Kit's love will heal your wounds, if you let it."

Another bald statement, not a question. Casey had the feeling Malama somehow knew all about Luke Trace. And Kit.

Determined to sell at least a crumb of their story to this woman, she plopped down on the bed beside Malama. "He's a hound when it comes to women," she blurted out, unable to stop herself. She meant

Luke, but it would be Kit's fingers she felt around her throat.

Malama looked at her, dark eyes twinkling. "This 'husband' of yours shows jealousy."

"He does?" she croaked, feeling her eyes grow round.

"James Dale is the hound." Malama adopted Casey's terminology matter-of-factly. "So, Kit touches you every time James comes near to let him know you are his *wahine*, his woman."

Casey decided to dodge that particular mine field and jumped up off the bed. She'd better get this conversation back on track fast. "Kit and I came here to try to...get used to each other, to reconcile our differences."

Malama's mysterious, knowing smile as she stood up made Casey flush. "Lokelani is perfect for lovers. Love your *kane*, your man, in the warm Lokelani nights, and this place will work its magic for you."

Casey was struck dumb until Malama took a step toward the door. With effort, she roused herself. "Oh, before you go, will you tell me the legend of Puhi?"

Malama reversed and dropped onto the bed, a puppet whose strings had been cut. "How do you know about Puhi?"

"Paul mentioned him briefly. He kind of...confided in Kit about what's going on. He said to ask you about the legend in private." Casey settled herself near the head of her bed, ready for a good ghost story.

Malama nodded, never taking her eyes off Casey's face. "Puhi was a shark god who lived in the sea. Long time ago now, the fisherman of Lokelani caught him in their nets. The kindest and gentlest of the fishermen fell out of his canoe. Puhi ate him up before the other men could rescue him."

Casey swallowed hard and grabbed a pillow to hug.

"And yet Puhi begged for mercy, asking the men to set him free. His excuse for eating the man was that, being a shark, he acted as a shark would act. The men agreed to free him on one condition. His spirit must take the human form of the man he killed and walk the land when the people of Lokelani need him. And so it is to this day."

It was a good ghost story, all right. Casey hung on Malama's every word while a healthy crop of gooseflesh sprung up on her arms.

Malama suddenly slapped her *muumuu*-covered leg with her hand before she stood up, making Casey squeak in alarm. "So you see, it could not be Puhi doing this. If he walks the land now, it is to protect us from those who are trying to frighten and harm us. I must go now, Casey. We have a luau tomorrow night."

After she saw Malama out, Casey pulled the draperies across the wide, screened doorways onto the *lanai* and verandah, and closed the connecting door. She didn't lock it.

She unpacked her sleep shirt, hung up her dresses, took a quick shower, and fell into bed, wanting nothing more than to sleep for a week. The last movements she remembered was tugging the clean, crisp sheet up over her then turning over onto her stomach. The last sound she heard was her own contented sigh.

The sensation of the bed moving beneath her woke her. She lay still, allowing consciousness to return slowly. Sleep hadn't been this deep or restful in months. Her brain registered that the light coming through the draperies wasn't nearly as bright as it had been. She wondered how long she'd been asleep.

"Luke?" She heard herself say the word, then she went quite still when she remembered the last time she had seen Luke. She cautiously rolled over, relieved to find it was Kit sitting on the edge of the bed, silently watching her.

"Try again. Sleeping on the job, Ward?" he asked, his eyes taking in her tousled hair and sleepy eyes.

He was relaxed, she heard it in the words. And his voice, well, she wouldn't mind riding that voice right back to dreamland.

"Recharging, boss," she said quietly, thankful that she hadn't done something silly, like scream, when she saw him sitting there.

"I can believe that. Did this Luke person ever tell you that you wake up real nice," he whispered to her.

She shook her head and smiled gently at him, then her eyes moved to the now-open door beside her bed. "Connecting door. You're not going to be a problem, are you, Kit?"

He grinned, his eyes warm as he leaned ever so slightly closer. "Heck no. Not unless you want me to be," he added, watching her closely.

She sensed a deep, abiding gentleness in this man. And most women would jump at the cautious invitation in those fascinating eyes. But Luke had made her wary, doubting her own judgment of men.

"Heck no, thanks anyway," she finally answered. "I've had cops up to here," she said, flopping one hand above her head onto the pillow.

He laughed and drew back. "I guess we have that reputation."

"Well earned. The job changes some men, makes them commit acts they wouldn't dream of if they were plumbers. By the way, what does your Significant Other think about you being here with another woman?"

He met her eyes, but his were unreadable. "I don't have a Significant Other to care one way or the other."

"Neither do I. Did you find out anything interesting?" she added as the silence between them lengthened.

"I found out I'm glad it's Paul sleeping in the barn with those bulls. Big. And they're isolated out there, wide open."

"I haven't been totally idle." She recounted the legend of Puhi.

He stood up and started to pace around the room. "So Malama thinks, like Paul, that someone is using the Puhi legend to scare those who believe it. Anything else?"

Casey sat up, Indian-fashion, with the sheet pulled up around her waist. "Yes. I'm afraid Malama is taking us in hand. She thinks a couple of nights of wild, abandoned passion together on Lokelani will fix us right up."

He smiled and looked away, reluctantly. "We'll worry about that later. Maybe Paul can help us there. Look, I hate to ask you to do this, but will you try to find out for me this evening just how much Jimbo wants to bring tours here?" He met her eyes again. "I don't think he'll need much encouraging."

She snorted. "The hand kissing on the verandah was just his knee-jerk reaction to a new woman on the scene, but his lunchtime display was to deliberately hurt Ilima. I think she really cares for him, poor kid." She sighed. "I'll play along, for tonight only, if you promise to rescue me before I have to pour someone's drink in his crotch."

He stopped beside the bed and looked down at her. "You would, wouldn't you?"

She grinned. "Believe it. And if he takes me seriously tonight, you'll have to help me find his 'Off' button."

"We'll find it. And trust me, I'll be keeping my eye on you from now on. Don't go away from the house alone, Casey. We're targets now like everyone else."

It was the first time he'd called her by her first name and she liked the way it sounded off his tongue.

He continued to study her, a disconcerting moment. She glanced pointedly at the clock on the nightstand. "It's time to get ready for dinner."

He took the hint and headed for the door between their rooms. "We'll keep this closed when we need privacy, but at night I want it wide open. And never locked. If I have to get to you in a hurry, I don't want to break down a door to do it. Understand?"

She felt a slow smile start. "And just why would you have to get to me in a hurry, boss?"

He shot her a crushing look. "Shark gods and marauding hounds come high on the list."

"One's dead and the other's stupid," she said solemnly then added softly, "Watch your back, Kit."

He turned and winked at her. "Heads up, Casey." Then he pulled the door closed behind him.

She had packed one special evening dress and two others that were basics. Jewelry and scarves would change their looks, as needed. She chose the basic long white halter gown, a pearl pendant and earrings, and a long, Hawaiian print chiffon scarf in shades of turquoise.

She swept her hair back from the sides of her face and held it in back with a pearl encrusted comb so that its loose waves hung down her bare shoulders in a cascade. A few tiny straps of white patent leather held high-heeled sandals on her silk-stockinged feet. She draped the scarf in the crooks of her elbows to pull up over her shoulders if she needed it later.

Kit had knocked on their door to tell her he was going on ahead without her, so she walked alone to the parlor doors on the *lanai*. The men were clustered in small conversational groups, but the buzz of conversation stopped when she stepped into the room.

Kit was at the bar talking to Paul and looking strikingly handsome in white slacks and a matching safari jacket. She saw him turn toward her, tearing himself away from the conversation to follow the direction of Paul's admiring stare. His face went slack with stunned amazement and his beautiful mouth opened slightly when her eyes locked with his.

As she took a hesitant step into the room, his eyes widened and his gaze dropped to the slit in her gown where a long length of tanned leg peeked through. She tensed involuntarily when she remembered that Luke had always told her she had beautiful legs. It was what attracted him to her in the first place, he'd said.

"*Aloha ahiahi*, good evening," Paul said heartily, coming out from behind the bar to greet her and usher her into the room.

She let her smile tell him she was grateful that he'd stepped into the gap, since her 'husband' was still gawking at her like a deer caught in someone's headlights. Paul shepherded her over to Kit before leaving them to check on everyone's drinks.

Kit held out a fat round glass to her. It trembled briefly. "I asked Paul to make it weak. It's a banana cow. I thought you might like to try it." His voice sounded hoarse.

The drink was a cloudy yellow liquid with a frothy white top and a perfect VandaOorchid perched on the rim.

She let him go on holding the glass while her eyes bored into his, and she hoped, out the back of his head since obviously there was nothing in between. "Well, you certainly didn't cover yourself with glory just now," she whispered furiously, glaring at him. "From now on we arrive together."

"Yes, dear," he said succinctly. "It's just that I didn't expect you to show up looking...like you do." His gaze drifted down over her again.

"You mean I clean up real nice, as well as wake up real nice?" she continued in a whisper that could peel paint. "Just what you ordered, according to your aunt. And I don't drink. Remember, dear?" She snatched the glass from his loose grip and took a gulp. "Ummm!" she said, in spite of herself.

He was standing up very straight, she noticed. "It's fairly harmless, which is more than I can say for that dress. James is hyperventilating."

"Your aunt's orders," she shot back. "Evening dress, she told me. Besides, isn't that my job tonight, to make him drool while I pump him for information?"

Kimo and Adam called to Kit from across the room, wanting his opinion in their discussion. "Yes, that is your job tonight, so sic'im," he said between clenched teeth.

She smiled sweetly up into his stormy face. "Well, hold onto your tight little Hawaiian butt, boss. By the time I'm through with him, I'll be able to tell you how he voted in the last election and what position he used the last time he had sex."

She watched him try to speak but no sound came out. Finally, he stalked off. As Kit moved away, James drew closer. Casey took the orchid from her drink and jammed it into the hair above her right ear just as James sidled up.

"Trouble in paradise? That's the wrong side, unless you're trying to send your husband a message." He reached out to pluck the flower from above her right ear and put it above her left.

She raised a hand to stop him, making full eye contact. "Let's leave it where it is for now."

She watched him swallow, hard. "Are you spoken for, Casey Kahana?" His voice was intimate but his eyes were alert.

Her two-inch heels brought her almost level with those blue eyes. Now might be the time to introduce him to the rules about leading on one woman and using another woman to hurt her. She'd have to make it right with Ilima later.

Her slow, one-shoulder shrug spoke volumes. "I can still enjoy the conversation and company of a handsome man for an evening, can't I?"

He smiled and placed a warm palm against her back to usher her to a quiet corner.

She glanced at Kit's group over her shoulder. The other two men were facing away from her and by simply raising his eyes, Kit could look over their heads in her direction.

Right now, his face was a study of conflicting emotions as he gave her a long look. She briefly saw dismay then anger mixed with something else when he glimpsed the expanse of her bare back, with James's caressing hand on it. Interesting.

"So, tell me about your work, James?" she asked when they were settled on a rattan love seat that was in full view of Kit and the room in general yet off to itself.

He leaned toward her, closing the gap between them. "My parents and I own a chain of travel agencies."

She shot another look out of the corner of her eye. Kimo and Adam were talking animatedly to each other. Kit had found something absolutely riveting on the ceiling. Very interesting.

"And do you lead tours all over the world?" She turned slightly sideways, leaning against the cushions and resting her left arm on the back of the love seat. He couldn't get any closer now unless he climbed into her lap.

He preened under her attention. "I sometimes lead tours. But I handle expansion and development, mostly."

"Then are you here on business or pleasure? Or shouldn't I ask?" She smiled and crossed one leg over the other, the slit in her gown parting to reveal a golden foot, calf, knee, and more than a hint of thigh.

They both looked up when a tinkling crash sounded across the room. Kit had dropped his drink. She raised her eyebrows at him enquiringly as he mopped his jacket front with a napkin. When Malama came to his rescue, she turned back to James. Very, very interesting.

"Oh, dear," she said with a breathy little laugh. "I can't take him anywhere. Now, should I have asked?"

James clenched one hand into a fist and used one finger of the other one to ease his collar and tie away from his throat. "I'm here for both but it was mostly business, until you arrived," he said smoothly.

She gave him a generic smile. "Go on, tell me about the business first," she urged.

"Well, I'm trying to convince Paul to allow us to bring small, specialized tours to Lokelani. We have elite, wealthy clientele who are interested in the unique aspects of the places they visit. For example, authentic Hawaiian luaus, like Malama's. You'll see what I mean tomorrow night."

She chanced another glance at Kit. Malama had him cornered, busily spraying his jacket front with the seltzer bottle while her mouth moved nonstop.

"I haven't been to a luau yet. It sounds like fun. So, has Paul agreed to your tours?" She took another sip of her drink. It really was quite nice.

He sent a hard look across the room to Paul. "Not yet." His jaws clenched on the words and a muscle worked beneath the smooth skin. "But he will. Soon."

Casey stared into the face of a stranger, and it wasn't a pleasant experience. An angry, immature young man lived behind James Dale's handsome, smooth-talking face.

She steered their conversation into other areas, including politics, until the dinner gong sounded. Kit was at her side before the echoes died away.

"Dinner. Dear," he added and glared at James before he took her by one elbow, hauled her to her feet, and hustled her away.

For the second time that evening she found herself in a man's hands when Kit placed one of his big, warm paws against her back to escort her. This touch felt tingly, definitely comforting, more than a little protecting, and most decidedly dangerous. Kit's fingers accomplished all those things while steady and unmoving against her bare skin. Still, she couldn't quite relax against them because of his insensitivity earlier.

The dining room was generously proportioned to accommodate an impressive matching mahogany table, chairs, and buffet. Casey and Kit were seated to their hosts' right. Kit got Kimo; Casey got Paul. On cue, Ilima carried in small plates on a tray and served them. She offered a hot glance to James and threw a cold one at Casey before she glided out of the room.

The *lomi-lomi* salmon, salted salmon that had been massaged, literally, with onion and tomato, was followed by Portuguese bean soup redolent with garlic and sausage.

Casey gave her full attention to Paul. If Kit was watching her, or James, she didn't want to know it. "How do you say 'tastes good' in Hawaiian?" she asked him.

"*Ono*," Paul answered with a smile.

"This is *ono*. I didn't realize Hawaii's cooking pot was as varied as her melting-pot culture."

"Each one is represented, from the early Polynesian voyagers, to the Portuguese, which is my heritage, to the Chinese and Japanese, to the *hapa haoles*, the half-Caucasian, golden-skinned people who are the end result."

Now, she glanced down the table at Kit. Her skin would never achieve the golden brown depths of his, but four months in the Hawaiian sun, even with protection, had given her a becoming tan.

Malama carried in a huge platter of spicy steak surrounded by taro, a potato-like vegetable, and chunks of pineapple. Paul explained that teriyaki-style, marinated in sugar and soy sauce, was a popular way to prepare meat in Hawaii.

Casey ate until she couldn't take another bite. Then Malama carried in and served a confection called macadamia nut pie. Casey managed a tiny sliver of the thick, creamy golden pie. It bristled with bits of macadamia nuts and was topped with a cloud of sweetened heavy cream that had been beaten with rum.

"All *pau*, finished, Casey?" Malama asked, smiling. "After Kona coffee you and Kit maybe take a walk? The moon is almost full. The beach is lovely in the moonlight." She ended with a wink that only Casey saw.

Follow the boss's lead, she reminded herself sternly, that's what he's paying you for. Kit nodded when her eyes sought his, so she agreed with a smile. She refused a second cup of coffee in the parlor and excused herself to go change.

In her room, she pulled on her turquoise tank-style swimsuit before she put on shorts, a T-shirt, and sandals. Kit called a greeting to her a few minutes later when he came into the room next door, with the same idea of changing clothes.

"Come over when you're ready," she replied in a lowered voice. She reached out with one foot and gently closed the connecting door.

She sat down Indian-fashion in the middle of her bed to wait. When he appeared, he wore cutoff denim shorts, a navy and white aloha shirt, and his running shoes. He also carried a black plastic flashlight that was big enough to double as a weapon.

"You won't need that with the moonlight."

"I want to take a look at the beach shack. That's where the clothes were taken from," he answered tonelessly.

They stepped out onto the verandah from her room. Kit's was the corner room and hers the second one in line on that side. He gave her a quick glance of surprise when, as they turned the corner to make their way to the steps, she took his hand.

"Someone's watching us from the parlor doorway," she whispered. A tall, slim body was in silhouette against the light. James.

Silently, they walked the beach path hand in hand, coming to a 'Y'. Off the right fork, the guest cottage—a medium-sized house, really—where Adam was staying, was visible amid the lush greenery of its own garden. Kit led her down the left fork.

Malama was right about the moonlight. Every step of the sandy, descending, twisting, narrow path was clearly visible, except where it was shadowed by lava rock. She pulled her hand out of his when they had to go in single file. Up and to the right on the *pali* the blades of wind turbines, which supplied the power for Lokelani Farms, pounded in the trade winds.

At the end of the path the beach and sea lay before them, a silver and blue dream, a half moon shape of pristine sand, gentle waves, and inviting emptiness. Casey's breath caught, then she kicked off her sandals and eagerly set out across the sand. Kit fell into step beside her, leaving his shoes beside hers.

She noticed a deep, three-walled hut facing the sea in the shadow of a line of spindly trees. When she asked about them, Kit explained that the casuarina trees, scrawny, gray-green evergreens with long needles, kept most of the sea spray from getting inland.

Dragging her mind back to tonight's assigned duties, she gave her report in a businesslike voice. "James is determined to bring tours here." She repeated their conversation for him. "I get the feeling he's dangerous, in a childish and self-centered way, when he's crossed or when he's prevented from getting what he wants. And I doubt he has many scruples. His behavior toward me, with my husband always close by, is evidence of that."

Kit gave a growl of laughter. "The less said about that, the better. Just warn me before you wear that dress again." The words had sharp edges.

Shock preceded anger. She came to a stop and let him walk on alone. When he realized she wasn't beside him, he turned around to see why.

Her voice brought down the temperature on the beach by several

wall. Anyone can get in there then just brush out the marks in the sand."

She was still too shell-shocked to react to the news. Not only were the effects of his kiss unexpected and long-lasting, they were unwelcome. She wouldn't trust herself to enter into a new relationship so soon, especially not with a man in law enforcement.

She offered no comment when they didn't find anyone on the path, but wondered silently if Kit had made it up. When he said good-night, she managed a thoughtful, "Hmmm," and left him standing on the verandah.

She did, however, find her voice after she showered and pulled down the sheets on her remade bed. Reclining against one pillow was a tiki, its wood cracked and black with age. Red feathers, bright as fresh blood, were tied around its neck with a piece of vine. Its sleek shark's head sported a mouthful of carved teeth.

The connecting door was open and she heard Kit's running approach at her first squeaky attempt at calling his name. He shot through the doorway and skidded to a halt on the wooden tiles, still wearing his cutoffs and nothing else.

"What? What's wrong?" he demanded, his eyes clinically examining her in her gecko sleep shirt, for blood, gaping wounds, or protruding knife handles, she guessed.

What, indeed? She momentarily forgot the tiki. She had noticed on the beaches that men of Hawaiian blood were remarkably free of body hair. Kit's chest looked sculpted and massive and as smooth and gleaming as tan satin...or a newly carved tiki.

He raised the volume when she didn't answer. "What? Or is this just a test of your early warning system?"

She dragged her eyes up to his face and pointed wordlessly at the bed.

"Well, well, two in one night," he said with a smile that gave her a chill. "This is either your welcome from Lokelani's prankster or a warning from Puhi, depending on which one you personally believe we're looking for."

Again, she found herself staring at him without speaking, but for a different reason. On the fleshy part of his right shoulder was a quarter-sized, perfect circle of lighter skin, still pink. She knew without asking that it was a bullet hole.

He picked up the tiki, looked under the pillows and the sheets, then turned to go. "Get some sleep. I'm going to wake you in a few hours to show you something special."

"E-Excuse me?" she asked, wide-eyed.
"A dead pig." He grinned at the look on her face then he left her.

Chapter 3

HER AWAKENING wasn't pleasant the next morning. She was pursued into consciousness by a dark, evil-looking tiki with red feathers around its neck. And two dead pigs. She rolled out of the comfortable bed and padded to the connecting door. Kit's bed was empty.

She pushed back the draperies from the *lanai* screen doors and concentrated on the flowers in the garden to erase the images in her head. Stretching herself lazily, she drank in the clear, pure light and the perfume from the flowers, overlaid with freshness.

"Good morning," Kit called softly, watching her from where he sat at the table on the *lanai*, outside the parlor.

Waving, she moved away from the screen. She splashed cold water on her face, pulled on and tied her blue silk kimono, which came to five inches above her knees, and went out in her bare feet. She noticed that Kit didn't pretend he wasn't watching her, eyes narrowed and a considering look on his face, as she walked toward him.

A plate of freshly cut pineapple, a pitcher of juice, a rack of toast, and a pot of Kona coffee sat on the table.

"Malama says she'll fix whatever you like." His eyes were warm, and prettier than the sky above their heads, she thought, as he looked at her from the top of her tousled hair to her bare toes.

"This will be fine." She dropped into a chair and looked at him earnestly. "Kit, did you wake me in the middle of the night and take me to a pit where there were two dead pigs...?" her voice trailed away when he laughed.

"I wanted you to see how the *kalua* pigs are prepared, in the old Hawaiian way."

She breathed a sigh of relief and buttered some toast. "Good. Thank you for showing me the *kalua* pigs last night."

As promised, or threatened, Kit had awakend her around three.

His upper body, legs, and feet were bare, but a *malo* cloth was wrapped around his lower body, like swimming trunks. She was alert enough to realize he did justice to the Hawaiian garb, or rather the lack of it.

She sleepily followed him as he led her on a silent, surrealistic journey in the moonlight to an area inland from the beach. He lifted her effortlessly down from the stile they had to cross, waking her up at last.

She became rooted to the spot when it appeared that Kit and Paul, who also wore a *malo* cloth, were preparing to bury two gaping corpses. Then she recognized the 'bodies' as being the carcasses of two lean young pigs, split from one end to the other, with the heads left intact. Relieved, she sat down to watch.

Using shovels, the two men tossed hot lava stones from a fire pit into the air and caught them again, to shake off any bits of dirt or sand that clung to them. The stones hissed when at last they were dumped into the cavities of raw flesh. A delicious aroma of sizzling meat filled the air.

"Is there anything I can do?" she asked at one point.

Paul held up a hand that brooked no argument, but he said kindly, "Only men prepare the foods that go into the *imu*, the underground oven, Casey. Later today Malama will prepare *laulau*, food wrapped in *ti* leaves, over a charcoal pit near the house. She might let you help, but don't count on it," he added with a grin.

She watched them place the pigs in a woven basket and lower it onto a layer of banana leaves and stalks. Scrubbed, leaf-wrapped yams were placed around them. They covered the pigs with hot stones and a layer of banana leaves, then more hot stones, more banana leaves, and finally, a layer of insulating earth.

Kit had walked with her, again wordlessly, back to the house, watching until she was safely inside. She fell asleep again immediately, still under the spell of the silent ritual she'd just observed.

Now, in the bright morning light, Kit fixed a cup of Kona coffee for her. She sensed that he watched her closely as she sipped it. When she shivered with delight then opened her eyes, he was staring at her with a dazed look on his face, his lips slightly parted. He swallowed hard and quickly looked away, tugging on his left earlobe. She picked up the coffeepot and topped off his cup.

He waited until she finished one slice of toast before he asked quietly, "Can you ride? Paul is giving us the grand tour this morning."

She, too, kept her voice low. "I can stay on, boss. I won't embarrass myself or you. Where's our friend from last night, the one who's a dentist's dream and has a weakness for red feathers?"

He grinned. “I have it with me. I want to show it to Malama, but the others were here until a little while ago. Our smoking friend was definitely Jimbo. I found cigarette butts on the path early this morning. They match his brand.” He gestured toward the ashtray on the table. “No sign of my flashlight,” he added in an aggrieved tone.

Malama suddenly materialized at Casey’s elbow, making her jump. Someone ought to put a bell on that woman, Casey thought to herself. It still amazed her how such a large woman moved without making a sound. Maybe she didn’t really touch the ground. Or maybe there were well-oiled wheels under those *muumuus* she wore.

Kit caught her eye and she sensed he was going to serve up the tiki. She braced herself as he simply brought it out from under his shirt and set it on the table. Malama made a little sound and slid down into one of the white wicker chairs. It creaked in protest.

“Puhi,” she whispered. “Where did you get this?”

Kit told her.

Her eyes glittered. “Someone is playing more tricks. Puhi would not do such things. My son Michael dressed as Puhi for the Aloha Week Parade many years ago.”

Casey’s eyes were glued to the black wood. A chill rippled over her, drawing Kit’s glance her way.

Malama stood up. “I am much troubled by this. I will take the tiki to the kitchen where Kimo will not see it. He is very frightened. I will ask Ilima about it.” She glanced at Casey meaningfully then glided away.

“She thinks Ilima might have done it? I’m confused. Do you have any idea yet as to what’s going on here, Kit?” She bit into a piece of juicy, sweet pineapple. It tasted nothing like those she had bought in grocery stores on the mainland

“Don’t just think what, Casey,” he said softly, “think of the why and the who. I think someone wants to force or frighten someone else into doing something. We’re spoiled for choice.”

He started to count off on his fingers, pausing to watch her suck the sticky pineapple juice off her own. When she was finished, he cleared his throat and began.

“We know it was James on the path and he wants to bring tours here. These pranks won’t necessarily achieve that end unless Kimo sells out to someone who might sway Paul, say like Jimbo and his parents. If Ilima put the tiki in your bed then we know one reason for that. Jimbo. Another might be that she’s working with Jimbo. Adam Hiroki seems to be a passive player but he might want a piece of this place for reasons of his own. Saito or one or both of the hands might work for anybody."

She sighed. "I see what you mean."

He looked at his watch. "Hurry up. I was just about to wake you when you wandered out. Paul is waiting at the stables by now. I'll meet you on the verandah."

When she presented herself fifteen minutes later outside the parlor, Kit nodded his approval of her snug jeans, long sleeved cotton shirt, leather gloves, and sturdy hiking boots. He had added a white cowboy hat to his jeans, hiking boots, and denim shirt. Somehow she had known Kit's hat would be white.

"I'll give you a quick layout of the island before we go." He pointed to their left. "The buildings and the grove follow the curve of the *pali*, the semicircle of the ancient volcano's cone. If you think of it as the face of a clock with the beach from eleven to one, then the house is at two o'clock, the bunkhouse at three, the stables at four, the grove from five to eight, the barn is at eight but inland, the airstrip is inland at nine, and the hangar is against the *pali* at ten." He pointed off to their right to a small white building. "That's a storage shed for sports equipment over there."

"Got it," she replied briskly, reaching for his hand. His fingers laced with hers as if they had been waiting.

They walked to the stables, past the bunkhouse where Saito and the hands lived. Saito stood in the doorway, holding a cup. He raised a hand in greeting. Casey felt her skin crawl and the hair on the back of her neck stand upright.

Kit gave her a searching look. "What's wrong?"

"Saito. He give me the creeps," she whispered.

"Probably just another admirer."

"No, it's not that simple. I don't think he likes me, and yet he—watches me."

"Most of the men around here do, including me. Or haven't you noticed?"

After that kiss last night, she noticed when Kit's eyes were on her, all right. They had arrived at the stables and she was saved from answering by Paul, who was leading two horses into the stable to be saddled.

"Which one is mine?" she asked brightly.

"This is Lady. She's sweet-tempered and gentle, aren't you, girl?" He patted the chestnut mare's neck. "I gave you Kuhio, Kit. Adam rode out earlier on Dancer. I ride Hilo."

Paul showed them the tack room and introduced them to the hands. Harry was young and cute as a button in his big cowboy hat, tight jeans, and fancy boots. Lono was in his mid-thirties and attractive in a swarthy kind of way. His hat was smaller, his jeans roomy, and his boots more serviceable. Both of them doffed their hats and called her 'ma'am' before they rode out.

Paul explained to Casey how to saddle a horse. Kit already knew what he was doing.

"I forgot to pack a hat," Casey whispered when Paul turned away.

Kit took one off a nail in the wall and put it on her head for size. "Woven from *lauhala* leaves. It's big for you but it will have to do."

Casey took it off. She pulled out the scarf that was holding back her hair, and tied it around the hat as a band. Bending from the waist, she filled the crown of the hat with the long swath of her hair, and pushed the hat onto her head as she stood upright.

"Now that's better," she said, smiling up at him.

"Much, much better," he said quietly while fire blazed in his eyes.

Casey's breath caught when his heaven-blue eyes glowed like blue sapphires from within the shadow of his hat brim. This job was turning out to be more of an adventure than she had ever imagined. And it didn't help matters, she reminded herself severely, when she allowed these feelings Kit aroused to bubble to the surface. She broke eye contact and turned to Lady.

Kit supervised her while she saddled her horse, closely examining the girth on the saddle before he threw it over Lady's back for her. He made her do the rest while he kept an eye on her.

Casey hoped, as she climbed aboard, that Lady lived up to her name and behaved like one. She had forgotten just how wide a horse was. They hadn't gone twenty feet before she was wishing she had been born with suction cups on her backside and legs.

"We'll stop at the grove first. The tool shed and the small holding warehouse are in the middle of it," Paul explained.

It was a pleasant little ride and Casey and Lady were getting along famously. They tied the horses to the wood posts of the fence beside the road. Kit hung his hat on his saddle horn, so Casey did the same.

"Our harvest season is September through January," Paul explained. "There are nuts all year long but not in quantity. We'll soon have enough for a shipment to Adam's candy factory in California. We ship some directly to companies like his while others go to processors."

Casey touched one of the dark green leathery leaves of a

macadamia nut tree. "How many trees do you have?"

"Three hundred trees on nine acres. We get about twelve tons of nuts from the grove in an average season. Because of the steady winds in the valley, our trees are only thirty-five to forty feet high. And they haven't needed any fertilizers, pesticides, or pruning, and no irrigation at all."

She stopped to listen to the soft plopping sounds around them. When she picked up a pod and removed the split leathery covering, she heard kernels rattling around inside the smooth light brown shells of the nuts.

"Don't try to crack them," Paul warned. "They're as hard as rocks. The processing companies use special equipment. Ask Malama to show you how she cracks the nuts she needs for her cooking and baking. She uses a special tool her son Michael made to hold the nuts while she cracks them with a hammer."

Kit took the nuts when she held them out to him. "How do you harvest them?"

"Strictly by hand. The pods fall when the nuts are ripe. The green husk splits open and has to be removed. In the off season, everybody pitches in to rake and burn the leaves and pick up and husk the nuts. It's optional for guests. In harvest time we have help."

Casey wanted to see and do it all. "We'll be glad to do our share."

Just then she stepped on one of the nuts Kit had thrown down. It rolled under her boot and would have sent her flying if Kit hadn't been behind her to catch her. He simply set her back on her feet.

"That's the biggest danger in the grove. Trust me, it's worse when you're wearing cowboy boots." A smile accompanied Paul's words.

They bent down to pass under some low hanging branches into another row of trees. The whole grove was shady and dappled with yellow-green light where the sun peeked through the leaves above.

Paul picked up a leathery green husk. "We feed the husks to the cattle. When the processors remove the shells, they sell them as ground cover or mulch."

Casey remembered the hard material on the driveway and around the plantings at the house. Meanwhile, she managed to step smack into a shallow box that had corn and grain in it.

"What's this?" she asked.

"Poison. Mice and rats are the biggest problem for all macadamia nut groves. This is how we control them instead of keeping cats."

When the men moved on, she tried to wipe her boot on the trunk of one of the trees. This wasn't her day.

"The shed is over here." Paul took a key out of his jeans pocket, opened the padlock, then put the key in his shirt pocket. He let the heavy door stand open because it was hot and dark inside.

"Saito and I were able to straighten some of the teeth on the rakes and replace the handles. We just took the rubber off the wheelbarrow tires that had been destroyed." He pointed to a corner.

The rake handles had been broken once, the splintered ends looking raw in the half-light. One rake head was so badly mangled that they hadn't tried to straighten it. Rubber from the wheelbarrow tires lay in a heap of tattered strips. The wheelbarrows themselves were dented and lopsided.

"Here's one of the saddle girths that was cut," Paul said with a sigh. "The cut was clean and went almost completely through the leather. It looked normal from the outside, but a little strain and..."

"Has anyone made an offer to buy Lokelani Farms?" Kit asked suddenly. "Anyone persistent?"

Paul shook his head. "Land developers and hotel chains have been after it for years, but not lately. As I said, Kimo is talking about selling out his share. I think Adam might be in the picture. I like having a partner but I'd prefer a working partner this time, though."

Kit put down the rake handle he'd been looking at. "How often does Adam come here?"

"A couple of times a year. But he didn't arrive for this visit until after all this started."

Suddenly a loud bang echoed off the walls and it grew dark. The door had blown shut. At least, Casey thought the wind had done it. She reconsidered when Kit knocked her down while diving across the shed. A scrabbling sound came from outside as someone flipped the hasp into place, put the padlock through, and clicked it closed.

Kit yelled a rude word and slammed against the wood door, but it was too late. They were locked inside. Casey decided to stay right where she was, on the floor, until her eyes adjusted to the darkness or until she figured out Kit's exact course. She heard him banging around, a loose cannon in the small area.

It was getting hotter inside the shed by the second. There were no cracks to look out of or to let air in, except a round window above her head. She knew they were in trouble.

Kit gave up and finally remembered her. "Casey, where are you? Did I hurt you?"

"Over here," she said, waving an arm above her head in the gloom. "And yes you hurt me but not where it will show."

Kit's big warm hand found her head then was joined by its fellow in making their way down to her shoulders. She gasped when he lifted her to her feet as if she weighed nothing at all. She was certain that if he had let go, she would have sailed right over his head.

"Are you sure?"

"Yes, I'm sure. There's a round window way up there," she said breathlessly and he let go of her.

He looked to where she was pointing. "That's not a window. It's more like a porthole."

"It is a large porthole," Paul said, coming over to join them. "It's from an old shipwreck. There's no glass in it, just plastic screening stapled onto the wood around its outside edge."

Casey studied it and their predicament. "If I stand on your shoulders, Kit, I can reach it. I'm narrower through the shoulders than Paul. I can push out the screen, wiggle through, and open the padlock from the outside."

Kit's voice wasn't encouraging. "And what about the drop to the ground? What's out there, Paul?"

"There's just bare dirt out the back, below the window. We put shale on the other three sides." His voice lowered. "But what if someone is still out there?"

Kit raised his voice. "Whoever did this better *not* be out there when I get out."

It dropped in volume dramatically with his next words, and a rawness came into it. "If you get hurt, my aunt will kill me. Take off those hiking boots," he ordered. "I'd rather have a foot inside a sock in my face than a foot inside a boot. Paul, spot for me. Get ready to help me catch her if she falls."

Kit leaned his butt against the wall under the porthole and bent forward, lacing his fingers together into a stirrup. "Left foot in here, hands on my head. On the count of three, push off with your right foot. I'll raise you up toward the window. Grab the edge of it and I'll try to put your feet on my shoulders."

"Please take it easy, Kit," she begged, suddenly thinking this wasn't such a brilliant idea after all. "I don't want to go into orbit."

It couldn't have worked better if they had practiced it, but the sensation of flying made her gasp. When her fingers closed over the bottom edge of the porthole, Kit grabbed her ankles, lifted, and slid her feet onto his shoulders.

"You might look slim, Casey, but you weigh a ton," he puffed.

She came right back. "That's my silver-tongued devil down there with you, Paul. Ever the flatterer."

The porthole was bigger than it appeared from below. She punched out the screen with one fist and stuck her head out. "I don't see anyone and there's nothing to break my fall, good or bad. I'm going out feet first."

Kit made a little sound from below her feet. "Be careful, Casey. If you can't do it and you're going to fall, just let it happen. I'll catch you."

She snorted. "How far has that line gotten you?" She heard Paul snicker in the gloom.

Gaining handholds on the outside of the upper edge of the porthole, she pulled her legs up and put her feet through the opening until she sat on the edge. Her blouse pulled up out of her jeans in the process. When she inched her way through the opening, she scraped her side painfully on a screw head. She turned around and hung from the bottom edge of the porthole, her body dangling down the outside of the building. Then she let go.

Bending her knees, she rolled with the landing. Still, the force knocked the breath right out of her. She sucked in deep gulps of the cooler air as she lay still for a minute where she finally came to rest. Accompanied by Kit's shouts of inquiry about her broken body, she picked herself up and dusted herself off.

"I'm all right," she called to him, gingerly exploring her burning side with one hand. Her fingers came away bloody. She cautiously made her way around to the front. No one was in sight.

When she reached for the padlock, she grinned broadly. "There's a problem, Sherlock," she said through the door. "Paul still has the key in his shirt pocket."

There was a pause. Paul's voice sounded sheepish through the thick wood. "I think there's just enough clearance to slide it under the door."

She'd bet Kit was mentally kicking himself. She still smiled, although her head both above and below her eyes had begun to pound painfully. Maybe macadamia nut trees didn't agree with her.

She unlocked the door, flung it wide open, and stood back. Kit pushed Paul out ahead of him. The three of them collapsed in separate heaps, but together in their misery, in the shale. Wind coming through the trees cooled them.

When Kit recovered enough to notice the blood on her hand and staining her shirt, he went off like a Fourth of July firecracker. Most of the curses were in Hawaiian so she didn't understand them. She noticed, however, that Paul looked mighty impressed.

When Kit paused for breath, she looked at him with bright eyes and a big grin. “No one’s ever talked dirty to me in Hawaiian before, Kit.”

Paul laughed, but Kit took a step toward her, his intentions written plainly on his face. He was ready to undress her to see how badly she was hurt. He didn’t calm down until she lifted her shirt to show him the gouge on her left side where the skin had been scraped off between the belt in her jeans and the band of her bra.

“It’s just a little scrape, Kit, and it won’t show, either,” she reassured him.

Chapter 4

THE MOVING air outside the shed felt wonderful. After Kit calmed down, she ventured back inside to retrieve her boots and sat down on the doorsill to put them on. Her head pounded again and she put her hands over her face for a second. When she raised her head, Paul and Kit were both staring at her.

"I'm fine. Really," she insisted. "And I had a tetanus booster two weeks before I came here. It's just a scrape. I bleed easily."

Kit looked unconvinced. "Paul, is there anyplace around here where we can clean up? I'd like to keep this whole episode quiet. Maybe someone will make a slip."

Paul gave a curt nod, a worried frown accompanying it. "There's a waterfall and a pool up ahead. Leave the road and follow the *pali*. Do you mind if I go back? I want to check on the bulls. The way you studied that map I showed you in the office, you should know your way around the island as good as I do. There's some soft ground farther ahead near the *pali*. Just follow the trail markers along there."

Kit nodded. "Keep your ears open. We'll be along later. Right now, let's get back to the horses." He took Casey's arm in a firm but gentle grip.

Paul was quiet for a few minutes. "Since we made the road over to Ohelo, that old *pali* trail I showed you on the map is private again and posted where it crosses over to the other side. The trail on the Ohelo side is falling apart. You might want to check out Lokelani's side sometime, though."

Kit was thoughtful. "The trailhead is before the waterfall, right?"

By that time they had reached the fence where the horses pulled at the grass. Casey was relieved to see they were still there.

"That's right. There's a beautiful little beach below, just before the trail crosses over. You can only get to it by the trail or from the sea. You and Casey could camp out there for a closer look," Paul added.

As soon as Paul mounted and left them, Kit made her show him her side again. "My aunt will kill me if she finds out I put a mark on you," he said as he turned her around and checked her other side.

She batted his hands away and let her shirt fall into place. "Stop making it sound like you paid a deposit on me. If I'm damaged when you return me, I promise you won't be charged more. Besides, how will she know unless I tell her or show her?" She paused and gave him a cocky grin. "Say, you better treat me right, boss."

When he opened his mouth to respond, she continued quickly. "Stop fussing, Kit. Just clean me up and I'll be as good as new."

They mounted and rode on. Long before they saw the waterfall, they heard it. A hundred feet of misty, white water tumbling over the edge of the *pali* above and crashing into a clear pool was worth waiting for, Casey decided at her first glimpse of it.

Kit reluctantly took himself off to look around, while she slipped out of her shirt, jeans, socks, and boots. She put the blouse to soak in a little pool then went into the water in her lacy white bra and matching bikini panties.

The scrape stung when it first got wet but the pain went away after a few minutes. When she got out, she scrubbed the blouse clean. By the time she finished, the sun and wind had dried her skin and her underthings were just damp. Kit had left a handkerchief for her to put over the seeping area when she got dressed. She tucked the wet shirt into her jeans to hold the dressing in place.

Kit's whistling as he returned made her smile. "It's all right, I'm dressed," she called out. His response wiped the smile off her face.

"I know. I watched you." He came to a halt in front of her, daring her to challenge his admission.

She did. "You watched me? You—"

"I said I'd collect the debt sometime, remember? And I'm not leaving you alone out here while I skulk behind a rock because you're afraid I'll see you in your lacy white bra and matching bikini panties. At least *you* weren't naked," he ended, a mulish look on his face.

She closed her eyes and counted to ten.

He waited until she opened them then asked, "Do you feel like going on?"

"Yes, I'll go on," she snapped. "Where are we going?"

"I think I can find that *pali* trail Paul was talking about. We have to backtrack."

They rode in the direction of the farm for a while then tied the horses to some brush. She certainly didn't see a sign of any trail on the *pali*, either at ground level or farther up.

Kit, muttering to himself, rooted around terrier-like at the base of the cliffs until he finally discovered the narrow path behind some bushes. It looked like it went straight up.

He gave her his hand, pulling her along behind him. It wasn't as steep as it looked and finally became a nice gradual climb, curving away from the valley below. The view was fantastic when it opened up between the plants that grew in profusion along the edge of the path. There were lots of loose rocks on the trail and an occasional open place where the trail edge wasn't overgrown. They stopped at one of them to rest and look around. She heard their waterfall again.

"Look up ahead, Casey," Kit said after only a minute. "The trail has been cleared." He took off.

She jumped up to follow him. He was right, from that point on, someone had definitely cut back the plants and vines that overran the trail and had cleared away the loose rocks to make it easier underfoot.

She stopped to study the trail ahead. "The plants along the edge were left standing as cover so you can't see the trail from below."

Kit brought a leaf to her. Half of it was gone, cut cleanly. "It looks like someone has been using the trail either from the Ohelo side or from that little beach Paul told us about. Ready to move on?"

The walking was definitely easier now as the trail leveled off more. She felt mist on her face and the roaring became louder as they walked. When they suddenly came upon the waterfall, she was delighted to find that it fell from higher above and the trail went behind it.

At one place, the wall of sparkling water sheeted down around them in a half circle. She stood quite still, thrilled by the illusion of standing within the shining water yet not getting wet.

"Lokelani is the most magical place I've ever been," she whispered reverently.

Kit's soft, deep voice came from behind her and above her right ear. "All of Lokelani is special, no doubt about it. And it's a dangerous place for people who want to keep themselves to themselves. More so for those of us who are finding it almost impossible to keep their hands off them."

He was standing so close she felt his body heat. It took all her self-control to keep from acting on either of two disastrous courses: burying herself in his arms in this enchanted place or taking off in full flight back to the horses. She managed to turn to him without touching him.

"Don't, Kit," she said raggedly. "Please. It's okay to be playful with each other, or to touch or kiss to carry this off. But I'm walking wounded right now and I suspect maybe you are too, emotionally, I mean. It wouldn't be fair to either of us to start a relationship because we're thrown together on Malama's Love Island."

He simply looked away and stepped aside, without speaking. She moved past him then knelt to retie her boot lace. There were puddles everywhere and the lace was dripping wet, slapping against her jeans every time she moved. Anything, at that moment, was preferable to looking into Kit's eyes.

But she didn't tie the lace, because her fingers froze in the act. In fact, she couldn't move at all. What she saw next to her boot riveted her to the spot.

"What's the matter?" Kit's voice was rough, the leg of his jeans just inches from her hair. "It's safe to get up now. My moment of weakness is past."

Casey gingerly picked up the dreaded object of interest then stood up. She walked over to where the trail came out from behind the waterfall. The light was better there. She peered at the object resting on her palm.

"Is this what I think it is?" She held her hand out to him, finally looking him in the eyes.

He whistled. "It's a shark tooth. A big one." He held the black triangle up to the light between two fingers. Its serrated edges were visible.

"How did it get up here?" She wasn't sure she wanted to know.

His eyes were still on the tooth. "Puhi. Or someone who wants us to think that." He put it in his pocket. "Let's keep going."

She paused briefly at the next open spot to enjoy the view while she finally took care of that untied lace. As she finished, a movement on the valley floor below caught her eye. It was a trotting, saddled horse. Riderless.

"Kit!" she whispered in horror. She felt rather than saw him come back to her and look where she was looking.

Down below, the horse was heading toward the farm. It was muddy up to its belly and its brown coat was blotched with a white lather of sweat. Kit took off back down the trail at a run.

"Careful! You'll break your neck!" she shouted after him, remembering the loose rocks and vines underfoot farther down.

They had gravity on their side this time and both of them went down the path a lot faster than they came up. And it was gravity Casey had to overcome when she tried to hoist herself up into Lady's saddle. Finally, she led her over to a rock and mounted from there. She followed Kit who had ridden off in the direction from which the horse had come. She caught up with him just as a figure staggered out from behind a fold of the *pali*, right in front of them.

"If that's Puhi," she muttered, "then he's been playing in the mud."

It took her another second to recognize Adam Hiroki. His white slacks and polo shirt weren't white anymore, and his new cologne would be the pungent smell of stagnant mud.

Kit dismounted and ran to him. "Are you okay, Adam? What happened?"

"Unless the trail has changed since I was here the last time, someone moved the trail markers." He wiped his face with a wet brown handkerchief.

Casey let Kit handle the situation. She dismounted and held the reins of both horses while she listened to the two men.

Adam sat down on a nearby rock and continued his story. "By the time I realized I didn't recognize where I was, the markers disappeared altogether. Soon Dancer was up to his shanks. I tried to stand up on the saddle and jump clear, unsuccessfully, as you can see. Dancer finally struggled out. I grabbed his reins just in time and he pulled me clear with him. Then he ran away. I hope he's all right."

"We saw him. He's probably at the stables by now. Casey, give Adam your horse and you ride double with me."

Adam dipped his head in acknowledgment when she handed him Lady's reins. His eyes didn't change, though, when he returned her smile. They were black and flat, with no emotion in them at all. She thought it had been a trick of the light yesterday when she first met him on the verandah, but they were in full daylight now.

Her head suddenly felt full and she wondered if it was from the rapid descent off the *pali* or just the beginning of one of those headaches that never came to fruition on Lokelani. "Go on ahead, Adam, if you're all right," Kit urged. "Get out of those wet clothes. We won't be far behind you."

They watched him ride off then Casey turned to Kit. "Well, we can add Adam to the list of victims."

Kit looked off in the direction Adam had come from. "Or it might have been meant for us and he got there first. Let's get back. We don't want to worry Paul any more than we have to."

Casey turned to Kuhio, Kit's huge mount. "How?" she asked,

opening both arms wide, encompassing his horse from one end to the other.

Kit's dimples appeared, catching her off guard. "Didn't you watch any old cowboy movies or ride double when you were growing up?" he asked as he put the cord of his hat over his head and let the hat hang down his back. "Mount as usual and I'll mount behind you. I get the reins and stirrups. Take off your hat or you'll have my chin rubbed raw with it."

"You'll have to help me. This guy is bigger than Lady." When he again bent over and laced his fingers into a stirrup, she added, "Be gentle, Kit, or I'll end up on the other side of him."

When she was secure in the saddle, he easily and gracefully swung up behind her like the *paniolo*, cowboy, he had been in the summers of his youth on his uncle's ranch. Casey sucked in her breath in alarm as both his arms came snugly around her. These seat belts of hard muscle would keep her from falling off, as would his broad chest which was tight up against her back.

He rested his hands on either side of the saddle horn she gripped in front of her "Sorry. Did I hurt your side?" he quickly asked.

She felt herself relax but grasped the excuse he handed to her. "It's all right now," she said a little breathlessly.

But it wasn't all right and it wasn't her side that bothered her. How could she feel so safe and content in his arms when she hardly knew him? The attraction they felt for each other was out in the open now, but this was still a business arrangement. Serious business. It would be up to her to keep it that way, she decided.

"I ought to send you back to Oahu, you know," he said in her ear. "I promised my aunt you wouldn't be in any danger. Now I'm not so sure. These pranks range from the ridiculous to the downright dangerous."

She swallowed the cocktail of fear, anger, and disappointment she felt at his first words. "You're the boss," she managed to say in a business-like voice. "I will, however, point out that you would still be parboiling in that shed if it wasn't for me. Or, you would have wrecked your injured shoulder trying to get out. And may I remind you who put her honor and integrity on the line last night, not to mention her body, to pump James Dale for you? And who found the shark tooth and saw Adam's horse today?"

"Enough!" His laughter communicated itself through her back. "In other words, you'd like to stay and help. Well, let's see what happens next. If I say go, you're gone. Do you understand?"

"Yes, boss," she said demurely.

After he stopped laughing, he was quiet for the rest of the ride. She was sure, however, that she felt him bury his face in her hair when the wind mingled her fair hair with his dark.

Adam was dismounting from Lady when they rode into the stable yard. Paul, Kimo, Saito, Lono, and Harry, who were gathered around Dancer, now gathered around Adam, except Harry. He stayed with the distressed horse while Adam described what happened. And only Saito raked her with a look from her head to her toes before he turned his attention back to the others.

"Puhi," he said when Adam finished his story.

Casey's eyes were drawn to his ugly tiki buckle when he said that. She saw Harry, the youngest of the hands, twitch. He led Dancer away and started to hose down his legs.

Paul had seen Harry's reaction, too, and spoke for his benefit. "Puhi is the guardian spirit of Lokelani Farms. He wouldn't do these things. It's a human devil we have to thank for these pranks."

Saito stepped forward. "How do you explain this? I found it at the foot of the *pali*." He held out a shark tooth, much smaller than the one they had found.

Kimo White lived up to his name, his face draining of blood beneath his deep skin tones. At that moment Adam asked his old friend for help and the two men left for the cottage.

Paul took the tooth from Saito. "I can't explain how this got there, Saito, but I want you and the men to concentrate on helping me find out what's going on instead of letting your fears and imaginations get the best of you."

Paul ushered Kit and Casey into the stables on the pretense of helping Casey unsaddle and tend to Lady.

"Has everyone been a victim of the pranks?" Kit asked Paul.

Paul sighed heavily. "Everyone has at least been touched by them. Ilima and James had their clothes stolen. The same for Kimo, and I suspect there's more that he isn't telling me about. When the tools were broken, it affected everybody except Malama. She doesn't do grove duty. Saito, Lono, and Harry had their saddle girths cut. The Jeep's tires being slashed affected Malama and me. She drives it over to Ohelo all the time. I use it to pick up guests at the airstrip or the dock."

While Paul talked, Kit unsaddled Kuhio, wiped him down, and picked up a currycomb. Casey watched him closely then repeated the steps for Lady. Harry was working on Dancer outside and was out of earshot.

Paul continued. "You lost a flashlight; Casey found the tiki in her bed. The three of us were locked in the shed. But everything that's happened here has had consequences for me, the controlling partner. Now, someone moved the trail markers. Maybe that one had your names on it and Adam simply stumbled into it."

Casey sighed. "Kit already thought of that. Sounds like everybody, all right."

"Whoever is doing this is stepping up the pace," Kit said. "Four of those incidents have happened in our first twenty-four hours here."

"Maybe there's a clock ticking somewhere," Casey observed. "Or maybe the bad guy knows you're here to stop him. I wonder if our wedding ring boxes are still in the pocket beside my seat in the plane."

Kit looked at her over Kuhio's back. "They're not. I checked last night after we did the *kalua* pigs."

At last they were finished. It was hot in the stables, despite the screened windows everywhere. She asked Kit if she could go snorkeling.

He was preoccupied. "I'll have to go with you. Get ready and I'll be along in a while. I want to show Paul what you found."

"Ask Malama for the key to the storage shed. That's where the sports equipment is kept. Kit and I padlocked it last night," Paul added grimly. "After he checked for the ring boxes in his plane."

IN HER ROOM, Casey changed her riding clothes for her swimsuit, pulling a clean cotton aloha shirt on over it, then went in search of Malama. She found her behind the house tending leaf-wrapped bundles of food in a charcoal pit. Malama kindly refused her offer to help and told her where to find the key and a stack of clean towels for the beach shack. She got the items from the kitchen then went to the shed.

Inside were bicycles, boogie boards, surf boards, lawn games, and snorkeling equipment, among other items. She took two sets of snorkels, masks, and swimming flippers and sat down on the verandah steps to wait for Kit. While she waited, she slathered on sunscreen and plaited her hair into a braid.

When Kit returned from the stables, he gave her a quick smile, approval in his eyes. He darted into his room, coming out again in seconds.

"I'll change in the shack," he said loudly from the verandah steps, his swimming trunks dangling from one finger. He lowered his voice. "That will give somebody a chance to steal my clothes."

He shoved some of the equipment under his right arm then pulled her to her feet with his left hand. He didn't let go when they started down the steps. "How would you like to camp out at that little beach Paul mentioned?"

"I'm in. When?"

"Can't go tonight because of the luau. Maybe tomorrow night. So, can you snorkel?"

She gave him a sideways glance and a slow grin. "I was hoping you would show me how."

She was an eager and willing pupil, and he taught her the basics of snorkeling in no time. When he was satisfied that she was ready, he took her out to the reef and the sea wall that filled in the coral.

Casey was in awe of the glorious sights that awaited her. The water was so clear that she felt it wasn't there between her and the colorful fish and rainbow-like coral. The only times her enjoyment was curtailed was when Kit withdrew from her to cast surreptitious glances toward the beach and shack.

They snorkeled until she was tired, then they leisurely made their way back to the beach. As she walked out of the water and up the sloping sand, a flash of light on the *pali*, above the tops of the casuarina trees, winked at her. It blinked again. Someone was watching them from up there.

She was ahead of Kit, so she turned around to face him, not an unpleasant sight. No doubt about it, Kit in his Olympic-style swimming briefs was almost as good as Kit in the buff.

"Come here, Sherlock, and bear with me. And remember this is business. You don't have to do anything, just listen," she said softly, putting her snorkeling gear on the sand.

He was immediately on alert, his gaze darting to each side of them briefly. "Business?"

She caught a glimpse of his surprised face when she stepped closer and put her arms loosely around his neck, bringing her lips close to his left ear. From up there, it would pass for an embrace.

He made it one when he sucked in his breath, dropped his gear, and wrapped his arms around her in a grip that molded her wet body against his. The sensations made her gasp.

"On the *pali*, a flash to the right of the waterfall," she whispered urgently, unable to pull away or to speak in a normal tone. She had to poke him in the back and repeat it before she felt his body tense with understanding.

His hold on her didn't lessen at all. "Looks like it might be on the *pali* trail near where it curves around to the other side." His voice was hoarse.

“But we just saw everyone not too long ago. I guess we’ve been down here a while, though. What should we do? I can go back to the house and do a quick head count while you check on Saito and the hands.” She managed to say all of it without whispering breathlessly, despite the fact that she suddenly wanted to throw him down on the sand and lick off his aftershave.

It didn’t help at all when he buried his face against the side of her neck, his lips moving on her skin when he spoke. “My trained, professional opinion is that we should stop talking. What if that guy up there reads lips?”

She pulled back and looked up at him, seeing laughter, and more, warm and willing, in his amazing eyes. “Damn you, Kit. After my sermon at the waterfall, I was trying so hard to be good.”

Then she kissed him until, she hoped, if someone called him Christopher, Chris, Kit, dear, Sherlock, or boss, he wouldn’t recognize or answer to any of them.

Chapter 5

A SOUND echoing off the *pali* near the dock brought both of them back down to earth. Outrigger canoes, motor boats, and fishing boats of some size were arriving. They headed to the house to shower and change.

Paul, whom they met on the path, told them that Saito was meeting the luau visitors at the dock, seeing that the boats were tied up in some kind of order, and sending the occupants on their way up the beach. Lono and Harry were assigned to the vehicles, bikes, and walkers arriving at the house from the Ohelo road around the *pali*.

"Saito, Lono, Harry, and Paul are accounted for. Let's have a quick look around when we get to the house." Kit wouldn't let go of her hand when they had to go single file on the path.

No effort at all was necessary. Adam and Kimo sat at the table on the *lanai*. Malama and Ilima tended the charcoal pit with James dancing attendance on a reserved Ilima. Way to go, girl, Casey silently cheered Ilima.

Casey glanced up at Kit who appeared lost in concentration. "That's everyone. Unless it was someone coming over the *pali* to the luau."

"My gut feeling tells me different. It's too late to do anything about it now with people everywhere. Meet me on the verandah when you're ready and we'll go down to the beach together."

After a shower, Casey looked through her wardrobe with dismay. In her travels through the malls of Honolulu, she had bought some aloha shirts and one *muumuu*, which she had left at home. Refusing to examine her reasons, she suddenly wanted to look special for this luau. The wraps Ilima wore all the time sprang to mind. She headed for the kitchen to ask Malama for help and found Ilima alone there. The girl started and Casey saw fear in her eyes.

She hesitated then smiled, hoping it was reassuring. "Help,

Ilima," she began, feeling a little uncomfortable herself. Did Ilima have a penchant for putting really ugly tikis in the beds of women her hound of a man lusted after?

She cleared her throat and continued. "I don't have anything to wear tonight except a couple of aloha shirts. I want to look special—for Kit. You always look fantastic in your sarongs..."

Ilima's face flushed becomingly before the girl spoke. "I have a turquoise flowered sarong that would look great on you," she offered shyly.

Casey heaved a sigh of relief. "Will you loan it to me and show me how to wrap it? Please? I've never been able to master a pareau over a bathing suit. If you wrap it for me, you might just save me from being arrested for indecent exposure later."

Ilima laughed, a surprisingly husky sound that Casey sensed would drive men to distraction. "I'll bring it to your room after I tell Malama."

In her bedroom, Casey took off her shorts, tank top, and bra and kicked off her sandals. Ilima helped her wrap the material snugly around her body, the two of them chattering the whole time. Casey saw Ilima pause when she noticed the raw area on her side, but the girl didn't comment and Casey didn't offer an explanation.

They were almost finished, so Casey knew it was time to broach the subject of James Dale. "About last night, Ilima," she began hesitantly. "Kit and I had a fight. I talked to James before dinner to take a breather from Kit—and to make him jealous. I apologize. I'm not looking for a new man, I promise you."

"I know," the girl said simply.

When Ilima solemnly continued her task, Casey couldn't help herself, blurting out what she really thought. "I didn't like it when James used me to hurt you when we first arrived. The man's a hound, Ilima. Are you really in love with him?" Despite her best efforts, her voice held a mixture of fascination and distaste.

Casey was surprised when the girl smiled and shrugged. "I thought I was. Malama told me how it would be, then you came and I saw."

"I'm so sorry, Ilima. James is pretty but he's flawed. Some men are like that. I know because I loved one once. You deserve someone who will love you and respect your feelings and what you give him."

This time shock raced through her at Ilima's reply.

"Now we love on my terms," the girl said simply. "Now we have an aloha love, meant to end when he leaves. He just doesn't know it yet."

By the time Ilima left her, Casey had no doubt that the lovely girl could take care of herself. Malama was in Ilima's corner, too. Between the two of them, James didn't stand a chance.

Casey was pleased with the end result she saw in the dressing table mirror. Her tanned shoulders and arms were bare, except for her hair flowing freely over her skin. A length of leg peeked out of the sarong's folds.

Hurriedly, she fixed a white hibiscus in her hair over her left ear and went out to meet Kit. He sat in the papa-san chair on the verandah near his sliding doors. He stood up when she slid her own door shut. He was wearing his *malo* cloth again with a matching aloha shirt hanging open. He looked good enough to eat. His swift intake of breath and her sudden awareness of his warm look through the half light told her she did, indeed, look special.

He took her hands and held her gaze with his own. "I'll be escorting the most beautiful woman on the beach tonight." With a sigh, he continued, "But that won't save us from having to carry food down there with us. No one escapes Malama."

They started down the beach path, hands and arms full, joining a moving line of people carrying mats, food, and anything else Malama had given them to transport to the sand.

When they got there, Paul introduced both of them and James to the workers who came to the grove every day in the height of the macadamia nut season and to the other residents of Ohelo. Adam, a regular visitor, simply renewed old acquaintances.

The workers had brought their families and Casey guessed the ages of the happy people on the beach to be from a few weeks to over eighty years. The workers were a lively group. Guitars and ukuleles appeared like magic and impromptu singing sessions, hulas, and chants took place. Torches pushed into the sand provided a circle of light as darkness fell.

Casey soon had so many leis around her neck that she couldn't turn her head, and their heady mixture of exotic fragrances made her dizzy. She gave some of them, with kisses, to the children she met.

She was aware that she drew more than one pair of male eyes as she moved through the crowd. Her own eyes searched out and followed Kit's blue and white *malo* cloth again and again. He was barefoot and shirtless now and wore a circlet of *maile* leaves on his dark head and a rope of them around his neck. To her, he looked like a Hawaiian god.

At Paul's shout, everyone went to the *imu* and watched as the pigs, tender to the point of falling in on themselves, were uncovered and lifted out. Malama supervised the orderly transfer of food from the charcoal pit to the beach. Just before the feast began, a band arrived from Kauai.

Casey sat down Indian-fashion on one of the woven mats on the sand, giving Kit a wide, grateful smile as he determinedly made a place for himself beside her.

"I've never eaten off a banana leaf before." She lifted the leaf and looked under it, hoping for a paper plate.

Malama's voice came from behind her. "No forks or spoons, either." She laughed as she covered their leaves with all kinds of food that looked and smelled great. "Use your fingers," she encouraged Casey before she moved on.

And Casey did, to eat such foods as *poi.* Kit showed her the one-finger and two-finger methods of getting the sour paste out of the bowl and into her mouth. Then she had *laulau* and *luau,* the mysterious leaf-wrapped food bundles from Malama's charcoal pit. Biting into a juicy pineapple spear, Casey took time out to look around her.

Glistening bodies and laughing faces were lit by torches, while tawny fingers tore apart food and delivered it to hungry mouths. She looked down at the crumbs sprinkling the fragrant, exotic flowers of her leis and clinging to her hands. Shrugging, she licked off her fingers one by one then reached for more pineapple. She had the whole ocean to wash in, after all.

The dancing began in earnest after the meal. The band played hulas back-to-back with the throbbing rhythms of the *tamure* and other South Sea island dances. She felt the warm, aware feeling of Kit's eyes on her as she watched first individuals then couples shimmying on the sand while she kept time with her hands on her knees. She poked him with her elbow when James and Ilima finished a wild dance and ran off, laughing together, into the night.

She was still staring after them when one of the older women danced over and held out her arms in invitation to Kit. Casey felt her jaw go slack, her lips parting, when he leaped agilely into the center of the circle of torch light and joined the woman in a energetic, erotic dance that drew the eyes of every woman present. No man should be able to move like that, she thought to herself.

Despite her determination to look away, she couldn't tear her gaze from his body, gleaming with perspiration and reflecting the torch flames. Her breath clogged her throat and she momentarily felt rooted to her spot on the mat when Kit slowly danced toward her, both arms outstretched, beckoning her to him. The closer he came, the wider her eyes grew, until her traitorous body just lifted itself off the mat, without her permission, and took his hands.

She had been to Hawaiian dance and chanting shows at The Shell in Kapiolani Park in Honolulu, so she knew the general moves and motions. So, when she found herself with Kit in the ring of light, she allowed the natural grace of the dance to take over, simply surrendering herself to the rhythm of the drums.

Slowly they circled each other, again and again. Then everything—the sounds of laughter, the chattering voices, the rolling waves—faded from her consciousness, except the flickering light from the torches thrust into the sand, the throb of the drums coursing through her veins, and Kit.

His eyes, locked with hers, drew her to him. Her hands left her hips, and her arms extended themselves to him in welcome as they danced closer to each other. They began to sink toward the sand. When they reached the lowest point of their descent, the drums stopped.

Casey gradually became aware of the silence around them and that they alone shared the dancing area. Then Kit took her hand and pulled her to her feet, and everyone seemed to take a breath or start to talk or laugh at the same time.

He took her back to her place on the mat then turned and walked off into the night. She watched him until the darkness swallowed him up, wanting to follow and let whatever happened simply happen. Instead, she sat quietly, knowing it was safer and saner, although it would take a little time to recover from the effects of the truck named Kit that had just bowled her right off her feet.

Casey watched the dancing for a while longer. When she was sure her knees wouldn't give way beneath her when she stood, she decided to go to the house to freshen up. Kit, Paul, Saito, Adam, and Kimo, surrounded by the hands and some of the grove workers, sat off to themselves around a small fire near the beach path, far from the light of the torches. She caught Kit's eye when she sat down on the sand in the shadows of the casuarina trees to listen.

"Well, starting tonight there will be a guard." Paul's no-nonsense tone carried to where she sat.

"A human guard will be useless against an angry *aumakua*," Saito growled.

Adam's slow, gentle voice was directed at Saito. "What would Puhi be angry about?"

Kimo tapped his pipe on a rock and began refilling it. His hands were shaking and his face was wet with sweat. He looked just plain scared.

Saito shrugged at Adam's words. He had an ugly, angry expression on his face. "I know I caught a glimpse of something near the *pali* and it wasn't human. Then I found that tooth."

"You and the men work out a schedule of watches," Paul ordered. "Count me in. Let me know when I'm on duty."

"And me." Kimo almost choked on the words.

Their conversation made her uneasy, so she slipped away up the path, leaving the laughter, the music, and the light behind. She needed to step back and think about the dance she and Kit had shared. It had been a revelation to her when she itched to follow him off into the night the way James had done with Ilima. Maybe it would be better if she went back to Oahu, as he had suggested, before she made another mistake.

James was strolling unsteadily down the path in the moonlight, his flowered aloha shirt open to the waist and his hair untidy, as if someone had run her fingers through it again and again. Ilima.

"*Aloha*, James. How are you this fine night?" she said by way of a friendly greeting.

"Think I'm in trouble, Casey Kahana. Think I'm in love." His words were slurred.

Now that was an interesting development, she thought to herself, but she wasn't following that conversational thread. She had problems of her own to consider in that area. "Think you're drunk, James. Things will be clearer in the morning. By the way, I see what you meant about Malama's luaus."

He was grinning, but he effectively blocked the narrow path without even trying. "Then you can't leave it this early."

She had seen Kit watching James when he pulled a flask out of his pocket and liberally laced his and Ilima's drinks. He explained that it was probably *okolehao*, potent *ti* root liquor. There were other flasks in evidence on the sand.

"Oh, I'm not leaving. I just want to clean up and clear my head. I'll go back in a little while." She tried to edge around him but he stepped in front of her.

She tensed. The self defense techniques Luke had taught her had gotten her into trouble the first and only time she used them—on him. How could she overcome her resulting fear from that encounter and use them now, if she had to?

"Have to pay the toll, Casey Kahana," he informed her, blinking and grinning.

Relieved, she sensed that he meant her no harm, so she smiled back. “And what might that be, James Dale?”

He thought for a long moment. “A kiss. Just a little one. Don’t tell Kit, though. Big devil. Please?” He swayed in a sudden breeze that blew up the path.

Poor James, doomed to love the chase and doomed to be alone at the end of it, she thought to herself. But at that moment he looked handsome and happy and his antics had put her in a good mood.

“Oh, James, you are pretty. It’s a shame you’re such a hound.”

“I know.” Sadness creeped into those two words.

So, she took his face between her hands and paid the toll, giving him a smacking kiss on the mouth.

“Thank you, my dear. You may pass.” He bowed and stepped aside, staggering.

She laughed again as she skipped past him. “Go sit down, James. You’re about to fall down.”

She hadn’t taken a dozen steps before the moon deserted her, just as a darker shape separated itself from the shadows. For one EKG, flat-line moment she understood the phrases ‘scared into fits’ and ‘scared to death,’ simultaneously. She only just managed to swallow her scream when Kit’s shape and voice emerged out of the nightmare in front of her.

“Didn’t I tell you not to walk around alone?” She wasn’t able to answer him yet and he took a step closer. “I asked why you’re—”

“I heard you the first time.” Her voice shook so badly that she scarcely recognized it. “Just let me finish this heart attack.”

During the short silence that followed, a sudden, all-encompassing anger cast a red haze over her surroundings. She swallowed a sob liberally laced with fear and anger. “Christopher Allan Kahana, if you ever scare me like that again, I will severely compromise your ability to father children. Personally.”

She reined in her emotions with difficulty. “As to why I’m out here alone, you went off to be with the boys, and I need to shake out my leis and wash off this pineapple juice. I’m sticking to everything.”

“Including James Dale, I noticed.” Until that moment she never realized that the human voice could convey fire and ice at the same time. “Just what the hell were you doing kissing him? Mrs. Kahana.”

At the realization that Kit had seen and heard their silliness, her face felt as if lava flowed beneath her skin. And the only explanation she had to offer, the truth, would sound silly, too, but offer it she must.

"I-I kissed him because he's happy drunk, and because he just shared a wonderful moment with Ilima, and because I felt sorry for him. For just a moment. For some reason," she finished lamely.

The fickle moon reappeared from behind cloud cover, bathing them in its light, enough light that she saw his eyes glitter.

"Let me see if I have this right." His carefully enunciated words and conversational tone made her squirm uneasily. "When I'm around, you want to find his 'Off' button. Yet the first time you meet him alone, you kiss him. Or maybe this isn't the first time you've met him alone."

She felt her mouth hanging open so she closed it. Her voice was a whisper as she glanced around to see if there was an audience she didn't know about. "Get a grip, Kit. You're doing the jealous husband act and there's no one around to see or hear. Last time I checked, I could kiss whomever I darn well please."

In an instant his big hands spanned her waist and they were like wallpaper and a wall. "Not when you're with me. As long as we're here together, you don't kiss anybody but me. Got it, Mrs. Kahana?"

She forced her voice past the unnerving mixture of shock, fear, anger, and satisfaction that his words brought. "Yes, Mr. Kahana, I've got it. Now take your hands off me before I stomp on your instep and gouge you in the eyes with my thumbs. Got it?"

She gasped in pain and surprise when his answer was to lift her straight up, without breaking a sweat, and put her down none too gently on the house side of the path.

He uttered one hurtful word and packed it in ice. "Tease."

Before her brain took in its meaning and its numbing hurt, her lips formed her return shot. "Cop," she whispered, and in her mouth it was a four-letter word.

They each turned and stalked away, him toward the beach, her toward the house.

He apparently had forgotten the scrape on her side and it beat and burned painfully now. But it was nothing compared to the pain in her heart. If she knew of a way off Lokelani that night with someone she trusted, she'd take it.

By the time she got back to her room, she didn't want to go back to the luau, didn't want to leave the door open between their rooms, didn't want to see or hear Kit Kahana again that night. She locked the connecting door, as well as the *lanai* and verandah screened doors.

In a misery of mind and body, she draped her leis over the bed posts and put Ilima's sarong material into the clothes hamper. After a quick shower, she put more antibiotic ointment on her side, took some aspirin, and went to bed.

KIT KICKED OPEN the connecting door at one a.m. She sat bolt upright, torn from a sound sleep and flung into the midst of a heart-pounding, panicked flashback. Her scrabbling fingers somehow found the switch on the lamp on her nightstand.

In two steps he was beside the bed, looming over her. She clutched the sheet to her, terror stifling her need to scream the house down. A sickening feeling of *déjà vu* engulfed her. Yet at the same time, from somewhere deep inside her, a tiny voice of reason tried to explain to her that this was Kit, not Luke. The message got through when she finally heard his voice.

"Damn it, Casey! I said I want that door left open at night—and never locked." The first few whispered words were forced between his clenched teeth.

So, her Hawaiian god aka tiki was pissed off about the door. She took a shuddering breath, gulping down the tears of reaction that were so, so close. She managed a scathing tone nicely, though. "Then don't close it on your way out."

She flopped over on her left side, away from him, cried out in pain, and sat upright again, finally angry. "And *you* can explain the broken lock to Paul."

She noticed he wasn't whispering now. "No problem. I'll even tell James about it. Personally. Why didn't you come back to the luau?" It was more of a demand than a question.

"Keep your voice down," she hissed. "I was tired and after you manhandled me, my side hurt."

"Oh, hell, I forgot. Let me see it. Is it infected?" He made the tiniest move toward her.

She shot back against the headboard, knowing her fear was again written plainly, if momentarily, on her face. "In your dreams, Kahana. No more touching. This marriage is over. I'm filing for divorce the minute we hit Honolulu. Then I can tease the whole uniform *and* plainclothes divisions of the HPD and you can't do a damn thing about it." To her horror her voice wobbled around the edges.

He seemed to deflate, all anger gone from his stance and his voice as he looked at her closely. "What's wrong with you? Casey, you know I didn't mean what I said. I was—"

She cut him off ruthlessly. "By the way, Ilima saw my side tonight when she helped me wrap my sarong. I hope she tells Malama that you abuse me."

"Well, it can be arranged!" He stomped back into his room, muttering strange, dark Hawaiian words.

The tears came in the darkness and she almost smothered herself to keep him from hearing. After it grew quiet on his side of the doorway, she lay calm but sleepless in the warm night, listening to the after-dark sounds carried on the soft breeze that moved through the screened doors on each side of the room.

She was in the middle of a long, involved thought about the person with the binoculars on the *pali* maybe just being a hiker or somebody when she felt herself falling asleep. Riding horses, being locked inside sheds, snorkeling for hours, luaus, and big fights with Kit must have that effect on her, she decided.

Her bedside clock read three a.m. when she got up to go to the bathroom. She stopped for a moment to look out the verandah door on her way back to bed. Wide awake now, she decided to step outside. Surely, her looking at the beautiful valley in the moonlight from the safety of the verandah wouldn't violate any of Kit's instructions.

She padded to the corner, leaned against the pillar there, and let her gaze move slowly across the vista before her.

Unfortunately, or fortunately, depending on which way she looked at it, her timing was perfect. A figure, dark against the reflected moonlight, slipped along the wall then went into the long, low building where the Lokelani plane, Adam's plane, and Kit's plane were hangared.

She ran back to her room, shoved her feet into sandals, and pulled on the shorts and tank top she'd shed earlier when Ilima helped her. Kit didn't answer when she called his name from the doorway, so she edged into the room.

He was sleeping on his stomach with lots of satiny tan skin showing in the tangle of sheets. She hoped a pair of underwear was in there somewhere. Again she called his name and got no response. Feeling urgency and, she admitted to herself, wanting the satisfaction of belting him while under the protection of that urgency, she slapped him hard on his sheet-covered butt and said his name again, louder.

He was on his feet, blinking at her one second after she saw him emerge from the flurry of sheets, one huge fist drawn back ready to knock her into the middle of next week. She squeaked in alarm and ducked.

"Casey? What the hell—?"

Briefs, not boxers, she noted before she spoke. "Get dressed. I just saw someone sneak into the hangar. I'll meet you on the verandah." She unlocked his door and went out into the night to wait for him.

She jumped when he came out behind her, still zipping up his cutoff shorts. He set down the small flashlight he carried and knelt to tie his running shoes. "Maybe it was Paul doing his rounds. He has the three to six watch."

She pictured in her mind the figure in silhouette against the building. "This guy was too tall to be Paul. And bulkier. Oh, and he was carrying something."

"Stay here," he ordered, jumping off the edge of the verandah.

She landed a second after he did. "No way, Kit. I saw him first."

His exasperated laugh rode the night breeze. "You're certifiably nuts, Casey. Does my aunt know?"

Keep it businesslike, she reminded herself sternly. Her voice was cool. "I thought you might break it to her gently. She's never seen the real me."

She heard the smile in his voice. "We can't take any of the vehicles and announce our departure to everyone on the farm and our arrival to the man in the hangar. Too bad we don't have the key to that," he added as they passed the storage shed.

Casey stopped in her tracks. "Wait! I forgot to lock it today when I put the snorkeling gear away. Maybe it's still open."

"That's my girl," Kit told her when the padlock slid off.

He wheeled out two bicycles. "It will be easier and quicker to use the road that cuts across the valley. We can lift them over the stile." They briefly circled to their right toward the beach and the closest gate and stile.

The moonlight was still bright enough that they didn't have to risk using the flashlight or the lights on the bikes. Unfortunately, the moonlight would also allow whoever was in there to see them, if he happened to look out.

A small door was cut into the edge of one of the hangar's big sliding doors, about six inches from its bottom edge. Kit plastered himself against the side of the building beside it and hesitated before he eased the small door open. It sounded like a cat with its tail caught in a winch.

"So much for surprising him. Stay low and go in fast," he whispered, quickly stepping inside with her in tow.

He yanked her aside so they weren't silhouetted in the doorway. Then he reached out and pulled the door closed.

Casey's nose wrinkled at the smell of engines and fuel inside. It was also very dark and very quiet.

"Use the flashlight," she whispered.

"Can't. It makes us sitting ducks," he whispered back.

"Then let's just turn on the lights. Maybe Paul will come. The more the merrier," she whispered, her hand on Kit's upper arm.

"Let's do that." She heard his hands make brushing sounds on the wood as he felt his way across the door to the wall. "Help me find the damn switch then stay down," he growled.

Casey turned around and brushed her way along for a few feet, ready to scream if her fingers encountered anything other than wall. She found the switch, warned Kit, then flipped it. Big fluorescent overheads blinked on, the planes gleaming in their light. Nothing moved as she crouched beneath the switch.

"Stay right there and watch the door. I'll look around," Kit said softly.

Casey felt limp with relief when Kit didn't find anybody or anything. He even looked inside the planes. When he was satisfied that the intruder was gone, he came back to her.

"He must have gone out the back while we were coming in the front. Paul and I will have to check the planes over carefully." He turned on his flashlight, telling her to turn off the lights.

They were halfway to the small door when they heard it. She jumped and felt Kit freeze beside her in the thick blackness that pushed against the small beam of his light.

She had heard chanting for the first time in The Shell in Kapiolani Park in Honolulu. A Malama-sized woman knelt on a woven mat. She slapped a hollow gourd with her hand then thumped the gourd on the mat to create a primitive rhythm. She chanted lovely Hawaiian words to that beat in a voice that changed by only a few notes. It was nice.

This chanting wasn't nice. This was a man's voice, low and echoing, that came from everywhere and nowhere. Each hair on her neck, arms, body, and scalp stood straight up on its root.

Kit moved first, jerking the light around to where he thought the sound was coming from, but the acoustics fooled the ear. The beam wasn't too steady and it got worse as he swung it around in a wide arc. It finally settled, steady as his Aunt Patty, on a walking arrangement of teeth.

Casey heard herself say a word that was sadly out of character for an executive secretary from Kahana Temps, and it came out sounding like someone was strangling her.

Puhi had a Hawaiian man's brown-skinned, hairless, well-muscled body that glistened in the light. There were circlets of green *maile* leaves around its wrists and ankles. It wore a gray *malo* cloth, like baggy underpants. Those were the good parts.

Where its head should have been was a horrible mask that bristled with large black shark teeth, as big as the one she'd found on the *pali*. The shiny dark eyes above fixed them with an icy cold stare. Around its neck, if it had one, was a necklace of smaller shark teeth with blood-red stones threaded between them. From somewhere behind all those teeth, it chanted. Then it took a step toward them.

"Lights, Casey!" Kit shouted at her and dove for the man-creature.

Disoriented, she screamed and backstepped until she hit wall. With both arms outstretched to find the switch, she watched the beam of Kit's light like his life depended on it. That little flashlight rolling around on the floor put on a light show worthy of the most unwashed rock group.

From what she heard and from the little that she saw, she guessed that Puhi was trained in the marshal arts. Kit was, too, but in his haste and in the darkness his forward momentum and weight were turned against him. He hit the concrete floor hard and he didn't move again. And in the ensuing silence his flashlight was switched off.

That was when Casey got serious about screaming. When they were kids, her brother teased her, saying she would never be defenseless as long as she could get her mouth open. These weren't just howls of terror and outrage, although some of those in there, too. The majority were words she didn't know she'd absorbed when Luke had the mean streets of LA in his mouth.

In the midst of it her frantic fingers found the light switch. She grabbed the first object she laid eyes on, a huge wrench, and turned to do battle with the monster that was hurting Kit.

Suddenly, as surely as she felt the cold metal in her hands, she realized she was alone except for Kit, who lay on his back, so quiet, so still. She dropped the wrench with a clang and ran to him, kneeling beside him to touch his face, her tears falling on his bare skin. When she raised her head from his chest where she listened for a heartbeat, his eyes were trying to focus on her.

"Don't move, Kit," she said raggedly, looking closely at his pupils.

"That was stupid," he said quite clearly then gasped. "My training...gone." When he caught his breath, he added in an accusing tone, "I thought you said you swear mildly."

"And I thought that thing was killing you." Her voice broke on the words and he looked at her with warm, intense, though slightly cross-eyed, interest.

The sound of an engine came from outside then a stumbling, clattering commotion at the door. Paul, followed by Saito a moment later, erupted into the building. She was insanely glad to see two pairs of feet and legs that wore jeans and boots, and with human heads attached.

What followed was a blur in her mind. Kit was all right, that got through the exhausted haze quite clearly. The wind had been knocked out of him and a huge lump blossomed on the back of his head from his poor landing.

Someone, Paul she thought, took her to Malama in the kitchen. Then Kit was there, too, like magic, with an ice pack on the back of his head. Saito, after taking note of her braless state, went back to the hangar to fit locks.

"There's another way out of there?" she heard Kit ask.

"There are several," Paul answered.

After that she lost the thread of their conversation. Over warm milk with honey and, she suspected, an added ingredient, Malama dragged out of her every last detail of Puhi, as Casey knew and loved him. She was numb with fatigue when she finished. She folded her arms on the table and rested her chin on them, watching Kit. He was looking at Malama and frowning.

Malama's face wore a strange expression, frightened yet puzzled at the same time. "The mask, a gray *malo* cloth," she muttered. "A shark tooth necklace with red stones."

"What are you thinking, Malama?" Paul asked, his tone troubled.

She simply shook her head, tight-lipped with silence, and refused to be budged. Malama was hiding something and everybody around that table was aware of it.

Casey felt Kit lift her in his arms to carry her to her bed, not caring that Paul and Malama watched them. "Come on, Mrs. Kahana. Get some sleep."

She snuggled against the warm skin of his chest and put her face against the side of his neck. "Don't drop me, Mr. Kahana, I won't bounce tonight."

"My arms and legs work fine, thank you." She felt his warm lips on her forehead when he put her down, slipped off her sandals, and covered her with the sheet. "Casey, wake up a minute." He shook her gently when she couldn't make her sleepy self answer.

She opened her eyes and looked up at him. He sat down on the edge of the bed and placed a hand on each side of her, leaning close. She felt no fear this time.

She spoke carefully. "Malama put something in my milk. That woman should come with a warning label."

He grinned. "Mine, too, only I think mine was a stimulant." His voice turned serious. "I'm sorry I hurt you tonight, er, last night, when I picked you up on the path. I forgot about your side. Is it really okay?"

She nodded. "It's just raw."

His voice took on a pleading note. "Casey, you just have to forgive me for what I said. You've handled me and this situation in your own unique way, but always with honesty and boundaries. And you've been an asset, just like you promised. A mean feeling came over me when I saw you kiss James Dale."

She swallowed the lump in her throat. "I'll accept your apology, if you'll accept mine for what I said. I just wanted to make you feel bad."

"It worked. I don't remember that one little word ever making me feel so—"

She raised her hand to his cheek, fighting to keep her eyes open. "I know and I'm sorry. It was a cheap shot. You deserve better. I have to keep reminding myself that you're not Luke."

His lips touched her palm briefly and she felt the bed move as he got up and moved away.

"Remind me not to go out on the verandah anymore in the middle of the night," she mumbled and was rewarded by his soft laugh from the connecting doorway.

Chapter 6

WHEN SHE finally surfaced late the next morning, she headed straight for the bathtub and a long soak, stopping only to pull the connecting door closed. Kit's bed was empty.

She let the hot, fragrant water work its magic then scrubbed herself from head to toe. The thick, soft towel, which she used vigorously, revived her almost as much as the bath had done. She pulled on her kimono, tied it loosely, and opened the bathroom door, body lotion bottle in hand.

She felt frozen to the wood tile floor when she found Saito standing in the middle of her bedroom. He didn't have the good grace to look guilty or ashamed when she glanced pointedly at the now wide-open connecting door behind him. His stare simply slid over her in that insulting way of his.

"What are you doing here?" She pulled her kimono more securely around her, suddenly conscious of her nakedness beneath the silk.

He held up one hand, while his eyes kept moving. In it were tools and a bolt lock. "Paul asked me to bring these to your...husband."

"Then please put them in his room and leave." She shifted uneasily.

He looked her over again with a half smile and jerked his head toward the doorway. "If he lets you get away with stuff like this then he's more of a fool than I thought. If it were me, you'd pay for this and I don't mean money."

Sudden, blinding anger washed over her like a wave at high tide. She allowed her contempt for him to run rampant in her next words. "So, you think pain and blood and bruising enhance the moment, do you? That doesn't surprise me. Listen, you Neanderthal—"

Just as Saito made a move toward her, Kit's cold voice cut her off and her gaze flew to the connecting doorway. His anger made him look bigger than he was. He filled the opening and his rage overflowed into the room.

"The games my wife and I play, or don't play, are none of your damned business, Saito. Now get out of here while you still have all the parts you crawled in with." His voice bespoke a savage anger barely held in check.

The look in his eyes, even at this distance, was enough to terrify her. When Kit took one step into the room, Saito retreated a step toward the *lanai* door. Then he seemed to recover. With a cold smile he threw the items on a chair and unlocked the door.

Kit's icy voice made him pause before he stepped through. "This is as close as you *ever* get to anything that belongs to me."

His words made her eyes open wider as she looked from him to Saito. But Saito had disappeared through the opening.

Kit slowly walked toward her, his eyes snagging hers so that she couldn't look away. But she could blush. She felt the heat to the roots of her hair. Bare-chested, he still wore his cutoffs. Somewhere in the long night, he'd taken off his shoes.

He stopped in front of her, his gaze dropping to the hollow of her throat where she felt her racing heartbeat throbbing beneath the skin. "I heard. Did he...touch...?" His voice wavered on the word.

A treacherous coldness crept into her, slithering along the long bones of her body and pulling the hot blood from her face. She last felt this mind-numbing iciness four and a half months ago, the night Luke....

She shook her head dumbly, watching him fight to let relief take the place of his residual anger and the adrenaline high that was chattering through him. *Please hold me, Kit*, she pleaded silently with her eyes. *Just hold me for a minute, or I'll never be warm again.*

"And you...you're naked under that, aren't you?" His voice was husky.

This time she jerked her head in a nod, still unable to speak. A shudder ripped through her and understanding finally dawned behind the fire in his eyes. He simply held out his arms and she fell into them, giving a little whimper as she did so.

He didn't take advantage of her moment of vulnerability, although she felt his physical response against her body. He simply held her like he would never let her go, until she stopped trembling and gasping and warmth replaced the cold.

"T-Tell Paul about him, Kit, before something terrible happens to a woman guest." She felt his head move against her hair as he nodded. "Did you get any sleep last night?"

This time he shook his head against her hair. “Malama wouldn’t let me go to sleep because of my bang on the head. And when Malama says you can’t sleep...”

“...you don’t sleep,” she finished for him.

“I’m going to catch a few hours now, though. Don’t go anywhere alone.” He put her away from him and she felt him sway with exhaustion. “Promise?”

“Yes, Kit. I’ll stay with Malama or Ilima until you come to find me. And thanks for checking on me when you did. Your timing was perfect. Go to sleep now. I promise I’ll be good.”

She kept the connecting door open while she dressed then cut through the courtyard to the kitchen for a bite to eat. When she asked how she could help, Malama handed her two pieces of fruit for breakfast and sent her to the grove with Ilima.

Ilima chattered nonstop as they walked to the grove, mostly about her family. “I have four brothers, big guys. I’m taking James to meet them soon,” she ended with a mischievous grin.

Casey was glad Ilima didn’t sense her discomfort as they approached the bunkhouse. She breathed a little easier when she saw that everything was quiet and nobody was around. Maybe in Ilima’s case, four ‘big-guy’ brothers and Malama’s presence acted as deterrents to Saito.

Still nervously aware of every sound and movement, Casey became caught up in the strange quiet that hung over the farm. It reminded her of the times she was in real trouble at home and had to wait all day for her dad to get home to deal with her.

Ilima, unaffected, showed her what to do in the grove. “Pick up the pods and pull off the green husks. The husks for the cattle go into one wheelbarrow, the nuts into another.”

Casey looked at the girl closely. Something was different about Ilima. Suddenly she saw what it was. Ilima now wore the plumeria blossom in her hair on the right side, meaning she was available. Casey smiled to herself, wondering if James had noticed.

The repetitious movements and quiet conversation soothed her. Soon they had a wheelbarrow full of husks and another of nuts.

“Come on, I’ll show you where we dump the husks,” Ilima said.

Ilima led her to a contraption attached to a section of fence. She dumped the husks into a hopper on a chute and flipped a switch. Over the din, she explained, “This special chute blows them over the fence into a trough for the cattle. Blowers are spaced all along the fence.”

“Hey, we have customers!” Casey pointed to the cattle loping up to the husks which were now on the other side of the protective fence.

They went back to the area they were working in. Now they raked the fallen leaves and branches that littered the grove floor and burned them in small fires, always standing by with rakes.

"Each day we go to a different part of the grove," Ilima explained. "It's not as boring that way."

They took their wheelbarrow full of nuts to the small warehouse in the grove where they dumped them into a wooden crate with 'Lokelani Farms Macadamia Nuts' stamped in red on the lid. Ilima reminded her that when she came with Kit she would have to get the keys from Malama.

"In season, when the crates are full, Saito nails down the lids and moves them to the warehouse on the dock. Since it's the off season, the crates stay here in the grove until we have enough for a shipment, this time to Mr. Hiroki's candy factory in California. In harvest season shipments go out all the time."

As they made their way out of the grove, Casey noticed James waiting for Ilima on the road. She cocked an eyebrow at the lovely young woman. "Some luau last night, huh?"

The girl nodded, smiling and looking up at Casey through her lashes. "Good luau. I heard about that dance of yours with Kit. You have some fun?"

Casey felt her face go hot. "We had a fight—but we made up. Broke a door in the process." She tacked on a grin. Let the girl make of that what she would.

Ilima laughed. "I'll be sorry to leave this place." At Casey's questioning look, she went on. "I've worked a few years to earn some money. I'm going to college soon. I want to be a teacher."

Would the girl never cease to surprise her? "Does James know this side of you?"

Ilima's smile was a little sad around the edges. "He doesn't want to know."

Casey almost said, "Poor James," aloud, because she was thinking it. The man was throwing away a diamond in Ilima.

Watching the young lovers walk away hand in hand in the noon sun, Casey wondered when James's ego would allow him to see that he was no longer the one in control of that relationship. She also wondered if he would learn anything from an 'aloha love' with Ilima.

Alone and uneasy, Casey turned away and hurried back to the house, almost running past the bunkhouse. Saito was nowhere to be seen and she didn't feel his eyes on her.

She took a short cut through the parlor to the *lanai* and the buffet lunch Malama provided daily. She stopped when she saw Kimo and Adam sitting at the table, leaning close together and talking. Since Adam's mud bath, they were like Siamese twins joined at the head. Kimo dug in his pocket. Casey dropped into a chair and grabbed a magazine to leaf through while she watched and listened.

"I found this where I left my clothes the day they were stolen from the beach shack," Kimo said to Adam. He put down a small shark tooth and she had the feeling he couldn't stand to touch it a moment longer. His hand shook.

Now she understood why Kimo looked so ill when Saito flashed the shark tooth he'd found.

He continued. "And I found that in my pocket this morning. I just reached in and there it was."

'It' was a tiki like the one she had found in her bed, only much smaller.

Adam's white slacks and polo shirt almost glowed in the shade. He sighed and shook his head. "It looks bad, my friend. Maybe another prayer stone at the *heiau?*"

"I-I've talked to Paul. He more or less agreed to consider what we discussed." Kimo wiped his forehead with a handkerchief.

"If you're sure, Kimo. Puhi played a trick on me, too, one that was worse than any he has played on you. Perhaps he doesn't want me to buy your share of Lokelani Farms."

A breeze wafted in through the screened door, bringing Adam's cologne with it. Immediately, Casey felt like someone had shoved a cotton ball up each nostril. When the men got up from the table, she rose in one smooth movement and dropped the magazine on the chair. She walked out onto the *lanai*, saying good afternoon to them as she went.

"Did you enjoy the luau last night, Mrs. Kahana?" Adam watched her with eyes that weren't quite as cold as usual and with an unexpectedly pleasant, if brief, smile.

In the midst of her surprise, she felt a grin start. "The whole night was...memorable, Mr. Hiroki." Let him make what he wants out of that, she decided.

He nodded slowly in an understanding way and went into the parlor with Kimo.

Paul motioned to her from the kitchen doorway. She was about to go to him when Kit came out onto the *lanai*, running his hands through his thick hair and gingerly rotating his right shoulder. Adam and Kimo were still talking in the parlor.

She walked over to him and linked her arm through his. His beautiful eyes looked like the map of a network of roads around two blue lakes. "Conference in the kitchen, dear," she purred.

"I feel like I've been hit by a truck," he mumbled as she steered him around the *lanai*.

Malama was ready for them with a private stash, a big pot of Kona coffee, a platter of sandwiches, and fresh fruit on the table. The door into the dining room was closed.

Casey poured a cup of Kona coffee and slid it in front of Kit before she poured one for herself. He shot her a grateful look as he picked it up with both hands.

Paul had just gotten up as well. "I finished checking out the planes. They're all right, as far as I can tell."

To Casey he said, "That's how I kept Kit awake the rest of last night, in the hangar. I told Saito to keep quiet about what happened."

Kit hadn't spoken yet but he had downed half of the cup of strong coffee. His hand went to his left earlobe and he tugged it. Casey had realized some time ago that this was an unconscious signal that meant his coffee was getting low. She refilled his cup then finished fixing her own, the first of the day.

Paul looked at Kit closely. "How's the head?"

Casey sipped the coffee's luscious richness, closing her eyes and shivering with delight. She opened them to find Kit staring at her, his chin propped on one hand.

"The head's fine," he finally said, dragging his eyes away from her. "Time to check out the *pali* trail and the beach, I think. Casey and I can leave as soon as we get packed up, if that's okay with you. Nobody but you and Malama need to know where we are. We'll be back tomorrow."

Paul smiled. "We'll tell everyone you're exploring Ohelo and staying at the B & B over there. I think we're in for bad weather soon. You'll have it timed just about right."

Casey let her mind wander between their words and those from the radio. Malama had it tuned, more or less, to a newscast from a Kauai station. The reception was poor. "No trace has been found of the priceless collection of jade stolen in a daring daylight armored car robbery a few days ago in Honolulu," the smooth voice said. So much for keeping a lid on that one, Officer Dan.

He went on to say that the police had noted that only collections of small objects had been taken in the four spectacular robberies that had been spread out over the past 24 months. Malama made little clicking noises with her tongue and shook her head as she listened at the kitchen sink.

Casey got up and went over for a quiet word with her about getting a liniment for Kit's shoulder. "I heard Adam and Kimo talking just now," she added. "What's a *heiau* and what are prayer stones?"

Malama's friendly face took on a serious expression. "A *heiau* is a sacred temple dedicated to one or more Hawaiian gods. When someone petitions a god, he prays there and leaves a stone wrapped in *ti* leaves. There's much *mana*, much power, there sometimes. Come, I'll show you one."

Casey gave Kit a shaka sign as they marched past and out the kitchen's verandah door. Malama led her to an old stone wall against the *pali*, behind the house. It was all that remained of an ancient *heiau*. There were four leaf-wrapped bundles on its top.

"Kimo's prayer stones?" she asked.

"And mine," Malama answered. "I pray for Michael's safety. Long time ago now a *kahuna*, a priest, blessed this ground. Nobody would lift a shovel to build this house on a once-holy place until it had been done."

Casey nodded her understanding and together they walked back to the house.

She and Kit set off as soon as they got themselves organized and as soon as Paul let them know that Saito and the hands were busy elsewhere. Malama packed food and Paul provided two backpacks. Casey forgot that they had to hike to the trailhead with their packs. Lady, wide as she was, would have looked good to her then.

The beginning of the trail didn't seem so steep this trip, and they reached the place where it leveled off in less time. Kit stopped behind the waterfall and pulled the little flashlight out of his pack, sweeping the wet ground with its beam.

When the beam stopped moving, Casey went over to him. The print of a bare foot was recorded in full detail in a muddy patch within the disk of light.

"Bare feet on this trail?" she asked in amazement.

"Our friend in the hangar last night was barefoot," he reminded her. "And what you saw him carrying was probably the big mask he wore for our benefit."

They moved on, slowly. They were on a part of the trail they hadn't explored yesterday. Here, too, someone had cut away the plants growing across the trail.

"Are there any caves up here?" Casey wondered out loud.

"Paul never comes up here but he thinks there's one. He says his father told him about it when he was a kid. You can see the whole farm from there. He thinks it's near where the trail forks."

When they reached the place where one part of the trail curved around the *pali* to the Ohelo side and the other down to the beach, Kit backtracked. He searched every nook and cranny of the uneven vertical folds of the cliffs. A sloped, pyramid-shaped rock that looked like its pointed top had been sliced off struck his fancy. When they climbed it, they were able to see all of Lokelani Farms and most of the trail, left and right.

"A perfect lookout to watch what's going on," Kit said. He pointed toward the beach at the farm. "It has to be near here where we saw the binoculars flash."

They turned as one to look down the back of the rock. At its bottom was a black hole.

Kit looked at her and grinned. "Am I good or what?"

"You're good, boss," she replied, a trained Kahana temp.

"Stay here," he ordered. "I saw it first," he added with another big grin.

He slid down the sloping back of the rock. Looking down the right side of the rock as she faced the cave opening, she saw a narrow space between it and the *pali*. One person at a time might get through that way to the cave's entrance, if he was able to find it from the trail. The cave itself was well-hidden.

Casey waited until Kit was clear then slid down after him. "It would be easy to climb to the top from this side to watch." She brushed off the back of her shorts.

"Do you listen to all your employers the way you listen to me?" he growled, flicking on his flashlight.

"You might need me," she replied with dignity. "To take notes or file something." She pulled out her flashlight as they went inside.

She followed close behind Kit, ready to use him as cover if they disturbed a colony of bats. It was dark and cool and dry. Nothing moved, which was good. Nothing squeaked, which was better.

Casey gave a low whistle when she saw what sat on the cave floor. There were lanterns, a sleeping bag, boxes of food and bottled water, a tiny gas stove, night-vision binoculars, regular binoculars, and a short-wave radio.

She was still gawking when she heard Kit make a little satisfied sound. She turned to him then jumped back, unable to stop herself.

Leaning against one wall and spotlighted in his flashlight beam was a mask with large shark teeth filling its gaping mouth. Above it, dangling from a root sticking out of the lava rock, was a long necklace of smaller shark teeth with red stones between them. The *malo* cloth, now a neatly folded piece of gray cloth, lay on a nearby rock. Kit flashed his light around the floor. It was crisscrossed with footprints of bare feet.

"A quick look around and we're out of here. You take that side of the cave and I'll take this side. Look for anything personal that might tell us who we're dealing with. Be sure to leave everything exactly the way you find it."

Her half included the Puhi outfit. She decided to leave it until last and, when she could no longer avoid it, she turned her light on the mask. A chill rippled over her. She hated to touch it but she had to. She lifted the mask away from its resting place.

It was carved out of one piece of lightweight wood and would fit right down over a man's head and rest on his shoulders. She guessed that he would look out of the mouth. No way was she going to try it on to find out. She inserted her light inside but there were no markings.

The rows of big shark teeth were glued into deep grooves slashed halfway around the head. One was missing, probably the one she found at the waterfall. The eyes were shiny black *kukui* nuts, like the hollowed out *kukui* nut ring on her finger, which had been her first purchase in her new home state.

The stones between the teeth on the necklace were bright red, maybe carnelian that had been tumbled to a high shine. The cloth was just a plain piece of gray material, the color of a shark.

She jumped when Kit touched her arm. "Find anything?"

"Puhi eats a lot of soup and canned macaroni products. It looks like he bought the food and water on Kauai. Nothing on the outfit. How about you?"

"Shorts, size 36 waist. Tank tops, size extra large. He sleeps in a sleeping bag that doesn't have his name on it. Neither do his binoculars or the other equipment. I can't get anything on the short-wave radio." Kit's forehead wrinkled in a frown. "He must take it outside on the rock to transmit. I copied down the frequency where it's set. It's a professional outfit."

He stopped and flashed his light around the whole cave one more time. She felt him willing the walls to give him the name and the reason for all this.

"We've done all we can do here, for now. Let's go to the beach and get some food." He headed for the entrance. "I'll have to watch this place tonight to see if Puhi comes home."

"Hold it, Sherlock." She was looking down at all the fancy wavy lines and blunt squares their hiking boots had left within the bare footprints on the dirt floor.

His beam of light followed hers and he swore. "I'll get a branch and we'll wipe them out."

"Not good enough." She grinned and trained her flashlight on his hiking boots. "I'll brush away our footprints, then the person whose feet are bigger than Puhi's will have to take off his boots and prance around in here barefoot. Remember, boss," she added primly, "we have to leave everything just the way we found it."

His answer was in Hawaiian but she was sure Kit was talking dirty again.

Chapter 7

HEAVING A great sigh, Kit sat down on a rock to take off his boots and socks. "I owe you, Casey." His eyes, boring into hers, were alight beneath the brim of his baseball cap.

His words took her thoughts back to that morning and her happy mood evaporated. "I think that was the point Saito was trying to get across this morning when you interrupted him."

He stood up, throwing his boots and socks outside the entrance. "Don't remind me. I'd like to go back down there and—" He broke off and swallowed his anger.

"I told Paul what happened. He has a soft spot for you, you know." He grinned then it faded. "Saito's days at Lokelani Farms are numbered whether he has anything to do with this mess or not. I asked Paul not to say or do anything about it until we get this sorted out. Just stay near me. Okay?"

She nodded then hurried outside to find some leafy branches. She used them to sweep, beginning in the farthest reaches of the cave and working toward the entrance. Kit traipsed around in the dirt, and whatever else falls on the floors of caves in Hawaii, until his tracks crisscrossed over and over again, like Puhi's had done.

They left by way of the narrow passage she nosed out between the rock and the *pali*. Once they were back on the trail, she handed him a steady supply of fresh leaves to clean off his feet. Unfortunately, the leaves turned his feet green. She bit back a big grin when he resignedly put his socks and boots back on his big green feet.

A little way beyond the cave, the path split. The fork on the left curved around the *pali* out of sight. Private property notices were posted prominently on both sides of the trail on the Ohelo side.

They walked that trail a little way. It hadn't been cleared and was falling away dangerously in spots. Naturally clear, the one bearing to the right on the Lokelani Farms side led to a lovely little cove with a beach that would make a travel agent's mouth water. There was a crescent of white sand and nice waves rolling in.

Kit gave them a pained look. "Boogie board stuff. The next time we come here, we'll bring the boards."

They opened bags of munchies to go with Malama's thick roasted pork sandwiches and got down to the business at hand.

"Are you going to try that frequency on Paul's short-wave radio?" she asked.

He nodded. "It would be interesting to see where the radio in the office is set right now, wouldn't it? Anybody can get to it."

She frowned. "Why would Puhi need a big set like that to transmit such a short distance. Walkie-talkies would do to transmit to the farm. Do you think Puhi is someone from the farm?"

Kit threw down two woven sleeping mats, too close together, on the sand. "There has to be two of them, one on the farm and Puhi. Everyone was accounted for at the farm when we saw the binoculars flash. And Puhi is spending a lot of time in the cave, even sleeping there. Somebody from the farm would be missed."

She crawled over and pulled one of the mats at least a yard away from the other. "But everyone at the farm had a prank pulled on them, including us and Adam, who got here just a couple of days before we did."

Gauging the new space between the mats, he cocked an eyebrow at her then threw a rolled up, lightweight blanket on each mat. "If you were doing this, wouldn't you include a prank for yourself so you wouldn't stand out?"

She chewed her lower lip in thought. "Good point. Okay, then maybe we can figure out which prank was a cover-up. For now, let's brainstorm. Who encourages the belief or believes deeply in Puhi in a fearful, negative way?"

"Saito, Kimo, Harry, probably Ilima, and, I think, Adam. I'd say we can eliminate Paul and Malama, and Lono seems to have his feet on the ground. Kimo and Saito are superstitious to begin with. Saito wears that tiki belt buckle all the time and Kimo wears a charm bag around his neck. Harry believes it. Adam, I think, plays father confessor to Kimo and his fears."

She repeated the exchange she overheard between Kimo and Adam earlier in the day. "Let's go back to why," she suggested, her brow furrowing in concentration. "What's the result of these Puhi pranks?"

"Adam might be Paul's new partner. Any of the others could be working for him or for someone else. Or, maybe there's something else going on that we don't know about."

"Could Kimo be doing it so he has an excuse for selling out?" she asked.

"He doesn't need an excuse. He's not ashamed of his beliefs, and their partnership agreement gives Paul first chance to buy Kimo's share. Paul has made it known by now that he wants another partner, but a working partner this time. I think we can leave out James at this point," he continued. "Kimo doesn't want his tours coming here. Adam doesn't either, from what I've overheard."

She hesitated before she voiced the thought. "Kit, it isn't Paul? He knows about the cave. He has ready access to the radio in the office. Maybe he comes under 'something else going on we don't know about.'"

He didn't react and that told her he'd considered it. "My gut instinct tells me no. Why am I here if it's Paul? He really wants a partner, but the right one this time. No, not Paul, unless a new angle turns up to change my mind."

She was relieved that Kit felt the same way she did about Paul. "I'm glad. Now why would Adam be interested in buying Kimo's share of Lokelani Farms?"

Kit brainstormed in cop talk. "He likes it here. It's worth a lot of money. He would ensure the supply of nuts for his candy factory, soon to be plural. I hear he's building a new one in Europe. Or, for an unknown reason, a hidden agenda."

Talking about Adam made Casey remember his cologne. Her nose reacted in sympathy. "You know, I just realized that I start a sinus headache every time I get near Adam and his cologne. As soon as he goes away, so does the headache. He must bathe in the stuff."

"Are you serious?" When she nodded, he added, "Tell me about the times you felt like that."

She thought for a moment then counted off on her fingers the times she recalled the feeling. "On the verandah when I met him the first time. When I handed Lady over to him to ride. And today when the wind carried it to me in the parlor. That's it. No, wait. I remember—" She looked at him, her eyes wide.

He waited, watching her. When she didn't go on, he said, "I'm a captive audience here. Would you like to share the revelation you're having?"

"It happened when I was unlocking the shed door," she said quietly. "And after, when I was sitting in the doorway putting on my boots. I put my hands over my face for a minute. Remember?"

"So Adam locked the door on us." He frowned. "Can you remember what we were talking about in the shed before the lights went out?"

"Let me think." She closed her eyes. "I'm good at this because of taking dictation. Paul was talking about Kimo selling out, that Adam was in the picture. You asked how often Adam visits. Paul said a couple of times a year but that he didn't arrive this time until after all this started. Slam!" When she opened her eyes, Kit was watching her.

"My aunt was right. You're good. Adam probably heard us talking about him in the shed and he locked us in when he had the chance. Then, because we reminded him that he needed a prank on himself for cover, he turned the prank that was set up for us, the moved trail markers, into one for himself. I think we have our cover-up prank. Good work."

She almost purred under his warm gaze. "But who's helping him or is he helping someone else?"

"The pranks started before he got here, so Puhi is his accomplice or his boss. We have to figure out who Puhi is and the motive." He glanced at the sky. "I know I promised you camping at the beach, but I really have to watch that cave tonight," he said with an apologetic look. "I won't leave you here alone. I'll go nuts up there if you don't come with me."

She looked around the little beach. As pretty as it was, she most certainly didn't want to stay there alone after everything that had happened to them so far.

"I'm with you, boss. Besides, if we're together, I can take a watch while you rest. We're both sleep deprived. We can divide the shift."

So, they took their mats and blankets, Casey's backpack, her hat, to cover her light hair in the moonlight, and a thermos of Kona coffee, and left everything else hidden on the beach behind some lava rocks. They found a concealed level place just off the beach path, near the top, where they were able to see the rock and the general area of the narrow passage beside it that led to the cave. From a sitting position and with the aid of the moonlight, the path up from the beach and the trail as it came around from Ohelo were also visible.

After they settled in, she watched Kit flexing and rotating his right shoulder over and over. "I asked Malama for some liniment for your shoulder. She makes it herself. I'll put some on for you, if you like," she whispered.

"Would you mind? After last night it's really stiffening up on me," he whispered back. He shrugged off his shirt while she got the lotion out of her backpack.

"Assume the position, please." She smiled to herself. "Relaxed, face down on your mat. Since I'll be concentrating on your shoulder, put your arms along your sides. I'll take the first watch, because you won't be able to stay awake through this, or I'm not my grandmother's protege. I'll wake you at two."

Her fingers tingled when she turned to him and saw that expanse of shoulders, as wide as the mat on which he lay.

"No exit wound," she observed, peering in the moonlight at the smooth skin on his right shoulder.

"Nope. They had to dig it out of me."

She couldn't resist, curiosity getting the better of her. "Kit, I've seen you with nothing on but your swimming briefs. I didn't see another scar. Where...?"

He sighed. "Stab wound, switchblade, left buttock. Hand to hand while resisting arrest. I take a lot of kidding about it."

"Ouch!" she said simply.

"By the way, it hurts since you manhandled me last night. Would you like to put some liniment—"

"I think not! But feel free to do it yourself when I've finished your shoulder."

She knelt on her mat and blanket beside him then warmed her hands by rubbing them together, just like her grandmother had taught her to do. She put some of the pleasantly scented liquid, still warm from the sun, on her palms and used gentle, sweeping strokes from the small of his back up and over his shoulders to apply it. Kit groaned.

"Sorry. Awkward angle here. Did I hurt you?"

He laughed. "Not in a bad way. Don't stop. Please," he begged.

For fifteen minutes she kneaded, chopped, stroked, and rubbed that unbelievably warm, satiny skin with its underlying, well-developed bumps, dips, and curves of muscle. She concentrated for five minutes exclusively on his right shoulder. Meanwhile Kit made little sounds of pleasure and satisfaction. Then she called a halt.

"You're enjoying this too much." And so am I, she added silently.

He moaned but didn't speak. Relaxed and pleased with herself, she turned her attention to her duties.

A short time into her watch, she found herself smiling. She was subjecting various parts of her body to poorly cushioned, prolonged contact with lava rock in the dead of night while she watched for a shark god, who really wasn't, to come back to a cave that had Kit's bare footprints all over its floor. She wondered what Patty Kahana would say about all this, especially about what her favorite temp felt for this gorgeous specimen of nephew sleeping soundly beside her.

She gently shook Kit at two o'clock, ready to duck if he came up swinging. He didn't. But he had no waking up period, probably because of stakeout duties. One moment he was asleep, the next he was wide awake. He rolled over and sat up, reaching for his shirt.

"That was—amazing. I'm almost afraid to ask," he whispered, "but where did you say you learned to do that?"

"Massage?" She smiled into the darkness, anticipating his reaction. "At my grandmother's knee. She was Swedish and a renowned masseuse. She taught me the magic."

She heard the smile in his voice. "Does my aunt know?"

"What do you think?" Suddenly she couldn't keep her eyes open. "I'm going to sleep now," she said around a yawn.

As she curled up on her mat and pulled the blanket up to her chest, she felt Kit's eyes follow her every move. She had the feeling his gaze would rest on her long after she was asleep, but she was too tired to appreciate the thought.

Puhi didn't show up for Kit either.

They went for a morning swim to wake themselves up then fried some eggs over a fire, packed up, and headed back to the farm. They didn't go inside the cave again, mostly because Kit refused to get black and green feet twice in one twenty-four hour period. Instead, he shone his light inside from the base of the rock. Nothing had been moved.

When they got to the house, they headed straight to the kitchen to get rid of the trash they had brought back with them and to check in with Malama. Paul was sitting at the table, having a cup of coffee. He looked more worried than ever.

"We lost a hand this morning. Harry quit. He said the place is cursed, but he wouldn't say what he saw or what happened to him."

"What was he doing this morning?" Kit asked.

"He did his stable chores, cleaned up a section of grove, then came to the house and quit. He wouldn't tell Saito or me why." Paul ran a hand through his hair.

Kit poured cups of coffee for Casey and himself. "We'll do a section of grove and see what we can find." He told Paul and Malama what they had found on the *pali.* Malama went very quiet.

During the long pause, when Kit should have been observing Malama's reaction, Casey sensed him watching her instead, sipping her morning coffee. She noted, when she opened her eyes after her third sip, that even Paul looked more cheerful.

He took up the conversation where it had broken off. "Well, be careful, both of you. I was just talking to Malama about asking Michael for some advice."

This stirred Malama from her reverie. "Michael is a policeman in Honolulu." Pride was evident in her voice.

Kit looked a surprised question at Paul.

Paul laughed. "A bit more than a policeman, Malama. He's with a state police special task force, no less."

"Not Mike Akoa?" Kit asked Malama. When she nodded, he added, "I worked with him several times. Nice guy. And good at his job. I hear he just got promoted."

Malama beamed. "I have to go to Ohelo later, to pick up James and Ilima. They went to see Ilima's family this morning. I'll call Michael. Tell him to come home for a visit. You want to come along?" she asked Casey.

Casey watched Kit tug on his left earlobe. She picked up the coffeepot and refilled his cup. He looked at her with a surprised, puzzled expression on his face.

Casey shook her head. "After the night we spent and after doing a section of grove, a nap is all I'll want. Thanks anyway," she said, stifling a yawn.

Kit and Paul talked about the mysterious watcher on the *pali*, aka Puhi, while Casey and Malama unpacked the remaining food from the backpacks. Malama's face was troubled when Casey described the mask and necklace, in more detail this time.

"Do you think this person dressed up as Puhi scared Harry?" Paul asked.

"Maybe he set up a prank, but he wasn't dressed as Puhi when he did. We watched all night." Kit looked a question at Casey.

"Who could fall asleep sitting up on a rock designed by Madame Pele? I'll carry the marks for a week, not that I'll be able to see them," she added with a smile.

Paul and Kit went to the office to take a look at the short-wave radio. When Kit came back, he shook his head at her. She got the keys to the tool shed and warehouse from Malama. They adjourned to their rooms, showered, and went to the grove.

Without incident, they made their way to a corner section. Casey showed Kit what to do and explained the blower chutes. He worked slowly because he looked around so much. They took turns tending the small fires to burn the debris. Finally, he took the nuts to the warehouse while she pushed their wheelbarrow full of husks to the closest chute in the fence.

There was one chute for every two sections in the grove. She had to walk through part of another section to get to their chute. Cattle watched her expectantly from outside the fence, waiting for the husks at the feeding trough that the chute emptied into.

But they didn't get her load of husks, and they hadn't gotten any of Harry's husks, either, by the looks of it. His wheelbarrow was tipped over, the green husks half in, half out of the hopper, spilling onto the ground around it.

Because a dead shark hung in one of the macadamia nut trees at the edge of the grove.

Casey had never seen a real shark before. It wasn't very big, but it was very dead. One milky eye held hers so that she couldn't look away. In fact, she didn't run or yell for Kit for a full minute. All she was capable of doing during that time was shift from one foot to the other and make little sounds in her throat.

That changed. She screamed Kit's name and started to run at the same time. Kit caught her in his arms when she plowed into him, full tilt, as he cut through a section of trees, closing in on her voice. His hands were on her shoulders while she told him what she'd found.

"Now we know what scared off Harry," he said after she led him back to the shark.

"Works for me." Her voice was shaking and she still held on to Kit's arm. "I'll give it a seven. Puhi chanting in the hangar was a ten."

"Let's clear up these husks then we'll tell Paul." His voice was grim. "He can get Saito to take care of our smelly friend." She heard satisfaction in that. "Then you get some rest. No arguments."

"You won't get any from me. Kahana Temps are trained not to argue with their bosses." She used her most precise voice.

"Hah!" He eyed her, long and hard. "But I promise I won't tell my aunt you like to 'debate' sometimes. I won't tell her you can swear like a stevedore, either. Or that your grandmother was a Swedish masseuse."

"Much appreciated, boss. Good reports are necessary for my continued success in my chosen field." She smiled at him primly.

His answer was a grin that set his dimples diving into his cheeks. He dropped a reassuring, affectionate, though exasperated, kiss on her forehead.

Oh, how she wanted to move, to turn it into a different kind of kiss entirely. And it wouldn't be her fault. She would blame it on the dimples. But she didn't move, because if she did, she could be surrounded by dead sharks, knee-deep in them in fact, and she wouldn't notice or care. When she was warm and safe and snug in Kit Kahana's arms, with his lips doing wonderful things against hers, nothing else mattered.

Now *that* was scary.

Chapter 8

SHE HAD a refreshing two-hour nap then persuaded Kit to take her snorkeling again. She let the warm water and the underwater beauty wash out of her memory last night's vigil and that day's jolt in the grove. Clouds were rolling in when Kit called a halt. He was in the lead as they threaded their way up the winding path from the beach, and she enjoyed the view.

Casey was just about to wonder aloud how Malama had made out with her call to Michael when she ran smack into Kit's back. He had stopped dead on the last sharp turn of the path. Before she could do so much as grunt, he whirled around and pushed her down behind a lava rock, his hand over her mouth. Amazed at how quickly and gracefully he moved, she didn't even bite him.

Kit pointed then brought his finger to his lips for silence. Saito was standing in front of the neat little wooden storage shed. Hunkering down, he peered under it. He also moved around behind it for a minute then walked away. Once he was out of sight, they looked under it, too.

"Something's blocking the light coming in from the back," Kit said.

They went around to see what was there. With a stick, Kit raked out a wad of material from beneath the building. He dug it apart.

"Oily rags, old sacks, and dried palm fronds?" she asked quietly.

Kit poked at the stuff with his stick. "I'd say someone is planning a fire."

She felt a surge of satisfaction. "We've got the sadistic little jerk."

Kit shrugged. "Maybe. Did he just now put this stuff here or did he just now find it here? He would say he was planning to watch the shed to see who sets fire to it. I guess I'll have to do the same tonight. I'm actually starting to enjoy the effects of sleep deprivation."

"Shouldn't we save the equipment inside?" she asked.

"Let's take out as much as we can and hide it behind the bushes." He rolled the dry stuff into a ball and shoved it back under the shed. "We'll probably have to leave the surfboards inside."

She knew by his voice that he thought *that* was a real crime. "We can move them and the bikes to the front, right inside the door, so we can save them if we have to." She grinned as she went around to unlock the shed door.

After they finished, Kit changed and went off with Paul. Heat, humidity, and clouds built up through late afternoon. Casey went to the kitchen and a subdued Malama allowed her to help with the evening meal.

By the time Kit knocked on the connecting door to escort her to the parlor, it was bucketing down rain and the wind was picking up.

She had chosen to wear her special dress that night. It was a layered chiffon confection of blues, from the lightest pastel to the deepest, vibrant tint. The skirt came to just above her knees and fluttered around her legs when she moved. Her hair was loose on her shoulders and she had sprayed orchid perfume at her throat, elbows, wrists, and behind her knees.

She invited him to come through. "Almost ready."

When he didn't say anything, she turned from where she stood looking into the half moon of mirror above the tall bureau. He had stopped in the doorway and was staring at her.

"You don't you like it? I thought you would because its your favorite color." Disappointment tinged her words, despite her best efforts.

"Oh, I like it all right," he said in a husky voice. "I like it a lot."

"Oh. Well, then. Thank you." Now she was utterly flustered and didn't know why.

"He must have been nuts. That LA cop. Totally nuts," he added in a bewildered tone.

She smiled at him and turned back to the mirror to put blue *paua* shell earrings in her earlobes. "Most of you big city cops are. I think it's the only way you get by."

He came up behind her and his eyes met hers in their reflection. They burned like blue flames.

She quickly looked away and held out the *paua* pendant that matched the earrings. "Make yourself useful. It's a nice big clasp, so you should be able to manage it."

When he brought the ends of the chain around her throat, she bowed her head and lifted her hair up so he could fasten the clasp. His lips were so soft and light on the back of her neck that she wasn't sure for a moment that he had touched her. Then her breath caught as fingers of fire crept through her. She let her hair fall back into place, murmuring thanks.

He stepped back but not nearly far enough. "You look and smell gorgeous, like one of our exotic Hawaiian flowers," he said softly.

Feeling an urgent need to defuse the moment before one of them did something stupid, she forced her voice into businesslike tones and spun around to face him. "Thanks, I needed that, boss." She hooked her arm through his, pulling him toward the *lanai.* "You'd need a flame thrower to get that shed to burn in this," she shared quietly when they were outside.

Music played in the parlor and James was sweeping a stone-faced Ilima around the room in an exaggerated dance. She had the feeling Malama had done a turn, too. Without a word, he neatly danced Ilima out of his arms and into Kit's then swept Casey away.

He'd been drinking. Heavily. His eyes were glassy and his tongue was thick. She could scarcely breathe because he held her so tightly.

"Heard the news? If you haven't, you're the only one. Paul turned me down flat," he informed her in injured tones. "Then Ilima 'splained to me the meaning of aloha love." She heard pain in his voice there. "What do you think of that, Casey Kahana?" He grinned but without a hint of humor in it.

Before she could answer, Casey saw two large, tawny hands close around the shoulders of James's white dinner jacket.

"I'm cutting in, James," she heard Kit say.

James let go of her with a grunt and a bewildered look when Kit squeezed and literally lifted him away from her, setting him down elsewhere. Then Kit neatly whirled her into his own gentle, protective arms, scarcely missing a beat of the music.

"Ilima has some nice hot coffee in the kitchen for you," he informed James over his shoulder.

She watched in wonder as Malama and Ilima lead James away. Kit calmly smiled down at her as if nothing untoward had happened.

"You amaze me sometimes, Kit."

"Good. That's important. I'm just glad to get it right occasionally." He quickly switched gears. "Now, do you see how susceptible men are to women who look like exotic tropical blossoms? Flowers have a very important job in the love life of plants, you know. They use their fragrance and color to attract—"

"He said Paul turned him down," she quickly interrupted before he rode that train of thought to the end, with her along as a passenger.

He gently pulled her closer, bringing his jaw to rest against the hair above her ear. "I heard," he said softly. "The evening is full of disappointments. Malama couldn't reach Michael. He's on special assignment. They wouldn't tell her where or get in touch with him for her because it wasn't an emergency."

Malama rang the gong as soon as the song ended. James was conspicuously absent from the dinner table. Ilima returned halfway through the meal to take over serving but disappeared again after serving dessert. They'd barely finished eating when they heard the rending screech of a tree falling nearby. Saito appeared in the verandah doorway almost before the sound had died away.

"Radio says it's a big one, headed this way, Paul." His gaze flicked over her, although his words were meant for Paul. "The stables and horses are okay. Need to batten down everything else, though. Lono and I could use some help."

Casey was on her feet a second after Kit. "I'll change," she said in his direction and headed for the *lanai* doors. She felt Saito's stare follow her out.

As she walked along the *lanai*, Paul's voice trailed after her, rattling off words like a Gatling gun. "Shut off the power, Saito. Everybody who's able to help, meet in the parlor as quickly as you can."

She heard Kit's running footsteps behind her then he ducked into his room. The connecting door still stood open and neither one of them bothered to close it.

"You can't come with us so don't ask," he said to the accompaniment of opening and closing drawers and closet doors.

She pulled on jeans. "I'd rather be outside in the dark with you than inside waiting for you."

He laughed. "We'll discuss that statement in detail at some other time."

Casey, punching her arms into a long-sleeved denim shirt, smiled but didn't answer him. The power cut out as she was tying her hiking boots.

When she went outside again, lanterns had been set up at intervals along the *lanai*. She bypassed the parlor for the mud room off the kitchen where she grabbed a bright yellow poncho from the long line of them hanging there. She took the biggest one she could find, a tan one, for Kit.

Casey saw that Malama had been on the move, amazing woman

that she was. Hot soup and coffee were coming to a simmer on a gas grill set up in a sheltered corner of the *lanai*. Already there were covered platters of sandwiches and cake on the dining room table when she cut through that room. Everyone was gathered in lantern light in the parlor.

Paul was talking to Adam and Kimo. "Your jobs will be to close the shutters on the house. Then help Malama in any way you can. She'll make sure there's plenty of hot food for everyone. Look after her and Ilima until we get back."

Kit looked around the circle of faces. "Where's James?" His question to Ilima cut through Adam and Kimo's whispered conversation. "Is he in his room?"

"Ilima?" Paul's voice held a note that made Casey swallow and shift in her chair.

The girl raised frightened eyes to Kit before looking at Paul. "N-No, he's not in his room. He was changing clothes when I took him his meal. He went out."

"Where, Ilima?" Kit's voice was quieter than Paul's but more intense.

She held Kit's gaze, pleading, sensing her exoneration lay with him. "We heard the tree fall. He said, 'If the storm is taking care of the grove, maybe it can take care of the other.'"

Paul's face blanched and he shot up out of his chair.

Ilima's voice rose hysterically and her eyes were on Paul now. "I don't know what he meant. He had *okolehao*. Don't be *huhu* with me." She ran to Malama and threw herself into waiting arms.

"I'm not angry with you, Ilima," Paul said over his shoulder as he made a move toward the verandah with Saito and Kit on his heels. "Lono, finish securing everything outside. Check the boats and make sure the cottage and bunkhouse are okay then come back here. Adam, you'll have to stay in the big house tonight. Saito and I will take the truck to the barn. Kit, bring the Jeep and follow us. We might have to split up."

Casey ran after them, pulling on her poncho and throwing Kit's to him. Each of the men grabbed a long, rubber, waterproof flashlight from a line of them standing on a table.

Kit turned and blocked her path while he shrugged on his poncho. He pulled the hood up over his broad-brimmed hat. "Where do you think you're going?"

"With you." She tried to dodge around him.

He stopped her with one hand. "If James turned out the bulls, it will be too dangerous."

"The bulls?" She swallowed hard. "But I want to help. I'll stay in the Jeep. I promise to do exactly what you tell me to do."

He hesitated then sighed. "Tonight's a good time to start." His voice dripped with reluctance. "Number one, stay close to me."

"Always, boss," she answered as she took a flashlight from the table.

Casey had no illusions about the bulls of Lokelani Farms, a near ton of muscle and bone each, that Kit had shown her in the barn. They were huge, deep-chested, and powerfully muscled, and beautiful in a dangerous way. The one chained in a stall with the sign 'Pilikia' on the gate had tossed his head and snorted, pawing at the straw with one massive hoof. The other, Hupo, had merely grunted and kept eating.

Saito was throwing thick, six-foot-long wooden poles and heavy ropes into the back of the truck when they got to the parking area beside the house. Thunder rolled, rain splashed down, and the wind howled as she and Kit threw themselves into the Jeep. She slid closer to him so the canopy protected her better. The Jeep leaped forward.

"This reminds me of *Jurassic Park*," she said in a nervous little whisper.

But Kit didn't answer, staring grimly ahead. And she was silent after that.

They braked to a skittish halt behind the truck near the barn. The double doors, the gate out of the yard, and the nearby gate in the fence were all dancing in the wind. James lay sprawled in the mud against the side of the building.

Paul and Saito ran inside while she and Kit went to James. He had passed out, a flask gripped in one hand. He appeared to be okay otherwise, after a quick once-over by Kit.

"They're gone," Paul said when he came out, after asking about James. "Look for tracks before they wash away."

The yard was churned with tracks so they spread out from the fence gate. Casey walked within sight of Kit, their powerful flashlight beams creating a wide swath of light.

"Here," Saito shouted at the same time their lights picked up a set of tracks.

"And here," Kit yelled.

Paul ran from Saito's set of tracks to theirs. "The tracks Saito found are bigger. Pilikia." He hunkered down to look more closely at the marks. "These are Hupo's, for sure. He's headed for cover near the *pali*, where the cattle will be. There are always a few strays outside the fence."

"Do you want us to go after him?" Kit asked.

"I can't ask you to do that. He's big but he's not mean," he added hopefully. "Saito and I can put James in the truck where he'll be safe and go after Pilikia."

"Tell us what to do with Hupo, Paul," Casey said in a tone that told him he didn't have to ask them.

He looked from one to the other a long moment before he made a decision. "First, you can't take the Jeep along the *pali*. You'll have to go on foot from here. And I know you already know this, Kit, but let me say it for my own peace of mind. Take a rope and one of the poles. Hook the pole to the ring in his nose and take him into one of the valleys. You can use the rope then to tie him to something. I don't think he'll give you any trouble. If he does, just get away from him. We'll try to follow once we find Pilikia and bring him back to the barn. You might be out here all night, though. Are you prepared for that?"

Kit gave one decisive nod. "And if you get back tonight, tell Malama we want James sober. I, for one, want a word with him." The tone of Kit's voice made her glad she wasn't the one who would be on the receiving end of Kit's word.

The fading tracks led them to a part of the *pali* she'd never seen before, beyond the now-raging waterfall they could hear but not see. She kept her head down and her light trained on the tracks while Kit used his to try to make out what was ahead.

The tracks finally disappeared, but they forged on, the flashlight beams reflecting off sheets of hissing rain. Casey lost track of time but it felt like hours that they sloshed ahead in the pelting rain and roaring darkness before a flash of lightning showed them what they were looking for.

When the lightning left them in darkness again, the beams of their lights reflected living eyes. A group of forlorn-looking cattle huddled together near the *pali*, taking shelter from it and comfort from each other's closeness. As they approached, the animals shuffled aside, revealing Hupo mired up to his chest in soft ground.

Kit made a comment in Hawaiian...earthy and colorful, she'd bet. She silently agreed as rain trickled down her neck and squished in her boots.

He examined the situation from all angles, talking calmly to the bull in a delicious whisper. Casey felt herself relax in response, although the words weren't directed at her. Then he efficiently fashioned a halter out of the rope and fitted it around the bull's head.

"You push, I'll pull," he shouted against a gust of wind.

Moaning to herself that she should never have promised to do what Kit told her this night, she waded into the thick, red mud. "Mud is good for the skin, mud is *very* good for the skin," she repeated as a mantra.

She put her shoulder against the bull's rump and her feet against a convenient rock sticking up at the edge of the mess.

"How come I get the end that smells?" she shouted at Kit.

Kit counted down and on three she pushed as hard as she could.

"He moved, Casey!"

"Okay, Hupo, work with me on this," she urged the bull.

She turned around, put her back against his rump, braced both feet on the rock, and pushed again when Kit told her to. This time she felt him move. On the next push, Hupo did the rest and pulled himself clear with a bellow of protest at the indignity of it all.

Casey sympathized with him. Without the support of the bull's body, she sat down in slow motion right in the mud, and there wasn't anything she could do about it. Hupo stood patiently and watched with interest while Kit pulled her out.

"He's staring at me," she said as she and Kit used their hands to scrape the slimy stuff off the back of her poncho and her jeans. She tried to stomp off the mud on her boots.

"No, *I* stare at you. He's just looking at that yellow poncho you're wearing. You take the lead and pick out a nice valley for the nice bull." Kit picked up the wooden pole, snapped it onto the ring in Hupo's nose, and led the bull by both the rope and the pole.

She groaned inside. She didn't want Hupo to be interested in her poncho or anything else about her. Yet, she admitted to herself, they couldn't stay out in the storm all night. Flashlight in hand, she walked in a wide circle to get on the *pali* side of Kit and the bull. Hupo shuffled around to keep her poncho in sight.

Some of the valleys at the base of the cliffs were just too narrow. She picked one of the bigger ones and quickly checked it out. When she was satisfied it would meet their needs, she led them through its brushy mouth, climbing a rock so they could pass her. The deep valley muffled the storm's fury and the rain fell more gently there.

They gathered brush and everything they could uproot and laid their booty across side-by-side formations of lava rock to make a roomy shelter for Hupo and another, smaller one close by for themselves.

Her teeth were chattering by the time they finished. She felt Kit shiver beside her when they climbed inside.

"We'll have to share our b-body heat."

"I h-haven't heard that line before."

"I just made it up. Is it working? Take off your poncho. We'll sit on yours and cover up with mine."

"I'm asking your a-aunt for h-hazardous duty pay." She spoke haltingly, her lips stiff with cold.

With much flapping and maneuvering inside their little shelter, they accomplished the feat. He put his left arm around her and she curled into him.

"H-How soon does this start to w-work?" she asked after a minute.

"Soon. Meanwhile, let's try this."

His cold mouth closed over hers, seeking her warmth as much as pleasure. In turn, she took warmth from him as they clung together. She pulled away first.

"Opportunist!" Her little laugh ended in a shudder. "S-Sorry, Kit."

He pulled her closer against him. "You're going to have to tell me sometime, Casey. All about the LA cop. You know that, don't you?"

She nodded. "But not yet."

Her shivering soon stopped in the warmth of his arms only to be replaced with exhaustion.

"Do you think they'll come for us tonight?" she asked sleepily.

"I doubt it. And how will they know where we are? We don't have anything to put outside the valley to tell them which one we're in."

"How about one of the flashlights?"

"We might need them later if Hupo decides to go for a midnight stroll. He's only humoring us." She felt him let his head rest back against the lava rock.

The silence was broken by the rain and little grunting sounds from the bull.

"Your aunt told me you're a nice man," she said against his shirt. "She was right. There have been times and situations through all this togetherness when you could have taken advantage. Thank you for taking it slow instead, Mr. Kahana, and for not letting me run."

His chest bucked with laughter. "My pleasure. Aunt Patty read me the riot act before she let me pick you up that morning, you know. And as for being a nice guy through all this, Mrs. Kahana, it's a good thing you can't read my mind."

She didn't know what to say so she said nothing at all. Smiling to herself, she went to sleep.

Chapter 9

A SOUND woke her as the first streaks of dawn heralded a beautiful, freshly washed day. She listened for the bull. Hupo had cooperated with them and still placidly munched on the plants that made up part of his roof. A shout broke the morning's stillness.

She moved her hand on Kit's chest and said his name. He still held her in his arms. "The cavalry has arrived," she said when he opened his eyes.

Another shout rang out and Kit answered. Untangling himself from her and the two ponchos, he ran to the mouth of the valley and hailed them.

"It's Paul and Saito on horseback, leading an extra horse," he yelled to her over his shoulder. "Hupo is okay," he assured the men, as they dismounted.

"How about you two?" Paul wanted to know.

As Casey folded up the ponchos she had dragged out of the shelter, she heard them talking about Pilikia and how he had been in a very bad mood by the time they found him last night.

Mud had dried on her jeans and boots and she brushed at them with her hands. Her hair felt flat and tangled. She bent from the waist, finger-combing and fluffing it with her fingers.

When she stood upright again it was to find Saito standing close, watching her. From the top of her head to the bottoms of her muddy boots, his eyes didn't miss anything. And she didn't like the look in them at all. She returned his stare until Paul's voice suddenly echoed in the little valley.

"Saito! See to the bull."

At that, he finally looked away, his mouth pulling up into a cold smile as he went to Hupo.

She sensed Kit beside her and looked at him. His fists were clenched at his sides and he shot a look into Saito's back that should have burned a hole in the denim shirt he wore. Then he turned to her, putting his body between her and Saito who was leading the bull out of its shelter.

"Are you okay?" His gaze moved over her face on a gentle journey. "No chills or sniffles after getting wet clear through last night?"

She shook her head. "You kept me snug and safe all night. Thanks for the body heat."

Warmth swirled through the sky-blue depths of his eyes. "Anytime, Mrs. Kahana." After a pause he added, "Let's get back. Jimbo should be stewed nicely in his own juices by now."

She and Kit rode double on Kuhio, the extra horse, while Paul and Saito dealt with Hupo. When they got back to the house, Kit didn't take time to change. She watched him usher a subdued James into Paul's office.

She showered then went to the kitchen for a bite and to consult Malama about the chances of saving her shirt, jeans, and boots. A good hour and a half passed before she heard the office door open. James, head down, walked past the kitchen's *lanai* doors. Kit followed a minute later, stopping to look in.

"Well, that cleared up a few questions," he said, coming inside when he saw her sitting at the table, cleaning her boots on newspapers spread over its top. He set down his missing flashlight in front of her before he pulled out a chair, swung it around, and sat astride it. He folded his arms across the back to watch her.

"Why did he do it?" Malama asked.

"*Okolehao*, immaturity, and stupidity, in equal parts. He was lucky Pilikia didn't kill him. Or that Paul didn't, when he got his hands on him."

"James is leaving tomorrow," Malama added softly.

"Following Ilima to Kauai is more like it. I think for the first time in his life, the hound is in love instead of in lust."

Shocked, Casey turned to Malama. "Ilima left?"

"I sent her for a visit to her aunt on Kauai. More better that way." She went into the laundry room to check on Casey's shirt and jeans, which were soaking.

Kit watched as Casey slathered leather cleaner on her boots for the second time. "Ilima put the tiki in your bed. She was trying to warn you off James."

She gave an unladylike snort. "She should have put it in his bed," she countered. "So he took your flashlight?"

"Returned with profuse apologies. And, of course, he turned the bulls loose. He says he didn't have anything to do with any of the other pranks."

"Do you believe him?'

"Yeah, I do. Trust me, I grilled him. I almost asked Malama for her rubber hose."

"So that means he isn't Adam's helper. It looks more and more like Saito's our man."

He frowned and nodded. "I have the nine to midnight watch tonight. Kimo has the midnight to three. Saito has the three to dawn."

She glanced at him and smiled. "Which means I'll be watching the shed from nine to midnight, and we'll be splitting the shift from midnight to dawn. These Lokelani nights are killing me. Sleeping in a bed is turning into a luxury, or a memory, I'm not sure which."

He rested his chin on his arms. "You're involved in this more deeply than I ever imagined when I asked Aunt Patty for help."

She stopped rubbing her boot to look at him. "I've been brain dead for months, Kit. I'm enjoying every minute of this adventure with you. These are nice people, most of them, and I'd like to help you stop whoever is doing this to them and to this beautiful, peaceful place."

"You've been a big help. I don't know what I'd have done without you a couple of times." He grinned wickedly. "Then there were a few times I didn't know what to do *with* you."

She felt a pleased smile curve her mouth. "Well, I can't just wait around the house for you to show up so I can drape myself artfully over you as your cover."

His look pinned her to her chair. "Oh, I don't mind. Drape anytime you feel the urge. It has its attractions, you know."

"So do naps, I'm discovering," she said, quickly looking away. "Will you take me to the beach later?"

He stood up, pivoted his chair around on one of its legs, and pushed it up to the table. "Wouldn't miss my daily dose of you in that bathing suit for anything. I'll be around when you're ready. Paul and I are going to cut up that mac tree that fell last night in the storm. Missed the fence, by the way."

THAT EVENING, Kit whistled appreciatively when he came to her room to walk her to the parlor. His eyes dwelt equally on her dress's low neckline and short skirt, but he simply offered her his arm without comment.

She wore her hair up that night, with curling tendrils feathering onto her neck and cheeks. Diamond-cut, heavy pieces of silver jewelry at her ears, wrists, and throat sparkled every time she moved, and real silk stockings caressed her legs when she walked. She wore two-inch black heels with her classic little black dress. The color seemed to match everyone's mood.

It certainly was a subdued group gathered in the parlor. Everyone spoke to James at some point, individually and quietly. He drank juice and kept to himself. Despite his actions in the past, Casey felt sorry for him.

"There's nothing more pitiful than a hound who's been laid low by love." She got to her feet. "I can't wait for it to happen to Luke, despite what he told me before I left. Back in a minute, Kit." She asked James to dance.

"Only with you on this night, and in this company, Casey Kahana," he said with a little smile.

Gentle mood music played on the sound system. James held her respectfully and talked quietly. She read him no lectures and gave him no pep talks, just a listening ear. Before their dance was over, she thought, just maybe, there was hope for him yet.

She felt Kit's eyes on her, as if he were touching her, the whole time she was in James's arms. When the song ended, she shook hands with James, wished him luck, and headed for the bar where she'd left Kit and her banana cow.

Kit intercepted her. "Dance?" he asked in a throaty whisper.

She felt uncertain. "Should we? I had the feeling Malama was waiting for us to stop so she can ring the gong."

He crooked an eyebrow at her. "This is Malama we're talking about here. Who do you think put the slow, romantic music on? This is all part of her plan, I'm sure."

He held out his hand to her and led her out into the middle of the room. When he took her in his arms, she went into them with a gentle smile. He rested his cheek against her hair as they moved slowly to the soft music.

"Time for some honesty," he said so only she heard. "You're playing merry hell with my sense of duty and purpose, Casey Ann Ward Kahana. All my senses, in fact. You're all I think about most of the time these days—and nights."

"Honesty, huh?" she answered breathlessly. "Then I can say that I know the feeling, Christopher Allan Kahana, aka Kit. Sometimes I can hardly keep my hands off you."

He pulled back to look at her. "What's stopping you? I promise I won't scream."

She laughed, in spite of the words she had to speak. "I haven't a few times, if you'll recall, and you didn't. Scream, that is." Her voice turned gentle. "Seriously, Kit, we have to keep a tight rein on this. I have a lot of emotional baggage left over from Luke, some things I haven't told anyone. I still want to take it slow, Malama and Lokelani considered. Please?"

"Now she wants to be sensible," he muttered to himself but against her ear so she heard him.

James went to his room to pack after dinner. Kimo and Adam played chess while Paul watched. A television was available for use with a VCR but nobody went near them.

She and Kit took on Malama for a killer game of Scrabble. Casey admitted to herself it was hopeless when Malama and Kit insisted Hawaiian words were legal, but she gave it her best shot anyway.

"I'll be leaving soon," she heard Adam say to Kimo. "Your hospitality has again made Lokelani Farms feel like home."

Casey caught Kit's eye then looked down at the board, while she listened shamelessly to the exchange.

Kimo took his pipe out of his mouth. "Soon it will be your home, my friend, and you can invite me to visit. If our plans meet with no objection." He turned expectantly to Paul.

Again, she glanced at Kit. He was watching them, a bland, expressionless look on his face that gave nothing away.

"Don't be too hasty, Kimo," Paul said. "There's a reason and a human hand behind everything that has happened here." He changed the subject before Kimo said anything else. "We have enough crates for a shipment for you, Adam. Are you sure you don't want them processed first?" Paul said the last with a fleeting smile.

Adam smiled coolly. "You will have your little joke, Paul, so I will explain again. The preparation of Lokelani macadamia nuts for our Dream Creams is a special process, a big secret. Please, make the usual shipment. When will it be?"

"Three days' time. Saito or I will take the crates over to Kauai to be shipped to Honolulu then to LA."

"Very good," Adam said.

Kit's eyes locked with hers.

At a quarter to nine Kit excused himself and went to change for his shift. She followed fifteen minutes later.

He called to her when she came into her room. "Don't turn on your light. Come here."

His room was dark. She stood in the connecting doorway. "Why? You don't have etchings in here you want to show me, do you?"

He laughed softly. "Another time. Wait a second." He threw open the verandah door draperies.

She saw him silhouetted against the moonlit darkness and walked toward him.

He kept his voice low. "The verandah is the best place to watch the shed, just a little way back from the corner, beside the papa-san chair."

She leaned against the door frame and put her face close to the screen to look where he pointed.

"It'll be in shadow in a little while and it's a clear shot to the shed," he continued. "Take some pillows to sit on. I want to keep moving on my watch, so you'll be there the full three hours. I'll check in, but I don't expect..." His voice drifted to a halt when he turned to her.

She looked up at him and heard him swallow. Hard.

"I, ah, I don't expect anything to happen this early," he finished, his voice rough.

"You should get going," she whispered. "Try to get a thermos of coffee for us from Malama on your travels."

"Sure. Coffee," he said in a strangely toneless voice.

And still they stood there, looking into each other's eyes in the moonlight until the tiny hairs on her body began to stand on end.

"Stop this, Kit. I'm going to change now," she said firmly, turning away from him.

"I think that would be a very good idea. Put on something that makes you look ugly." And he was gone.

By the time she changed her dress for shorts, a tank top, and sandals, moonlight had cast her hiding place into deep shadow. She threw down her bed pillows, sans cases, and sat down on the verandah floor, as instructed, a little way back from the corner where Kit's room formed one front corner of the house. Beside her, giving her cover, was the big rattan papa-san chair.

A gentle breeze blew and the sky was full of stars. If Saito was watching the shed, she didn't see him. She saw Kimo once. He stood at the corner of the verandah, smoking his pipe, unaware of her presence. He glanced around quickly then beat it back into the house. She'd bet that, when he had the watch, his 'rounds' never took him far from the safety of the verandah.

Kit checked in about ninety minutes later, coming by way of his room and bearing a thermos of coffee, some bananas, and the kitchen fire extinguisher. They said very little and he disappeared into the night again. He joined her at midnight, sitting on her second pillow, and she went inside for a rest stop.

After that, they sat quietly and sipped coffee. She was right about Kimo. He did his midnight-to-three watch sporadically from the verandah.

Around two o'clock in the morning, a dam was breached inside Kit and words flooded out of him. Stories about his time on the police force and how he got his wounds came first. Then he told her in a whisper about the beautiful Hawaiian girl named Mei, whom he had loved, and how she died in a boating accident two years ago at the very moment he was on his way to her house with a diamond ring.

She reached over and twined her fingers with his when she heard the pain in his voice. "Oh, Kit. I'm so sorry," she said brokenly, but she wasn't able to reciprocate, to willingly immerse herself again in the pain of her own memories.

He was silent for a while, then he said softly but with a steely resolve in his voice, "You're not getting off that easily, Casey. It's time for you to unpack that emotional baggage you're carrying around inside you. Show it the light of day, or rather the moonlight of this night, then show it the door. You—*We* can't go forward until you do."

He was right. She admitted it to herself at the same time she admitted that she very much wanted to go forward with Kit. She drew up her knees against her chest and wrapped her arms around them, rolling herself into a tight little ball. And yet, hesitantly, she leaned into him so the words she was about to whisper wouldn't carry. He welcomed her and held her loosely against him.

In that moment she realized how important it was for her to tell the story, not just to anyone, but to Christopher Allan Kahana. She took a deep, shuddery breath and tried to put into words what she had relived in her mind a hundred times but never spoke of, not even to the counselors at the battered women's shelter where she volunteered.

"Six months ago, I found out by accident that Luke was seeing another woman. When I confronted him, he admitted it. He said he had dated others while we were engaged, that it was just the way he was made. I didn't know if any of them had a ring. I knew I did. There were no tears, there was no shouting. I just handed it to him and told him I never wanted to see him again, that I couldn't love where I didn't trust."

When she tried to continue, her voice shook so badly that she had to begin again. "We never lived together. We had keys to each other's apartments and cars, but I wouldn't take that step without marriage and we had put off marriage, both of us. One of the reasons I hesitated was that I noticed changes in Luke. He was drinking more and he was often angry."

Kit shifted ever so slightly, reminding her that he was a cop, too, reminding her that he'd probably seen other men change the way Luke had.

"I thought he'd returned all my keys until one night six weeks later I heard a key in the lock. I had the chain on but Luke simply karate kicked the door and popped it out of the wood. And there he was, very drunk and very angry, in my living room. I was sitting on the couch in my night clothes, reading."

She felt Kit's arms tighten around her until he held her in a fierce embrace. "There was no reasoning with him. He just kept saying he loved me and he-he wanted to show me, as if making love would make everything all right between us. Then it got ugly. When he started tearing at my clothes, I used one of the self defense techniques he'd taught me. It worked and that made him more angry. Then it got uglier. He slapped me."

Kit made a little sound, deep in his throat, that let her know he was sharing her pain.

"I was bleeding where my teeth cut the inside of my mouth. I landed on the floor beside an end table where I kept a heavy paperweight. When he came at me again, I opened his head with it. I ran to a neighbor's door and called his partner to come and get Luke's sorry ass out of my life. I wouldn't press charges if he wouldn't."

"Oh, Casey," Kit whispered.

"I spent the night with a friend. She took me to the hospital to be checked out. That's why I had a tetanus booster right before I came here. The next morning, I had a steel door installed and the locks changed at my place, and I made some decisions. Over the next two weeks I gave notice at my job, sublet the apartment and contents, sold my car to another friend, packed my clothes, transferred my bank accounts, and made my plane reservation. One way. I always wanted to visit Hawaii, now I was going to live here. I didn't run away exactly, but there was a lot to be said for all that water between me and this stranger I once loved."

"Did he try to see you again?" Kit's voice was furry with emotion.

"My bags were in the car; I was leaving it at the airport for my friend to pick up. Luke called, begging me to forgive him and to meet him on neutral ground, his mother's house. He said he realized how much he loved me and that he wanted another chance. So did I, but not with him. It was too late. He had killed my trust in him in every way. I said one word to him. No. I hung up, drove to the airport, and boarded my plane. That's how I ended up in a Honolulu hotel room with just my clothes and no job prospects and a Honolulu telephone directory."

His heart thundered beneath her cheek when she finished. She felt his lips against her hair.

"Oh, Casey, I've made some mistakes with you. Forgive me. I apologize for kicking open the connecting door the night of the luau. I must have terrified you. And I'm sorry it took me so long to realize what you needed from me that morning Saito was in your room."

She heard herself make a little mewing sound against his T-shirt.

"But I want you to remember what I'm about to say and be very sure about it, no matter what happens or doesn't happen between us. *I'm not Luke*. The only way I'll ever physically hurt you is if I accidentally step on you or something. And I'm really glad you liked the way Kahana looked in the phone book. Okay?"

"Okay." She cried just a little then and he comforted her, then they were quiet together.

He squeezed her fingers in warning when they heard Saito and Kimo talking on the steps of the verandah at three, the changing of the guard.

Saito was taking the job seriously, or pretending to. They heard him say he had checked the grove, the warehouse and tool shed in the grove, and the stables before he came on watch. Now, he said, he was going to check the boats, the airstrip, and hangar. Kimo simply said goodnight and went inside.

It started to cloud up and the moon played hide and seek as they watched Saito head toward the beach path. She saw a flash from his belt buckle as he turned to glance back at the house.

A short while later Kit whispered in her ear, "I have to go inside for a minute."

He had just disappeared into his room when she leaned forward, alert. Had there been a movement near the shed, or was it just a new shadow caused by clouds skipping across the moon? Nothing happened, so she relaxed. Hungry, she reached for a banana. Maybe food would help her concentrate on sorting out the shadows.

In another moment she had no doubts about what she was seeing. Flames licked up the back of the storage shed.

Forgetting to swallow, she jumped to her feet and tried to call Kit's name around the mouthful of fruit. She spit it out and grabbed the fire extinguisher. Screaming Kit's name, she jumped off the edge of the verandah and ran toward the shed.

Then she saw something that made her feel like she was wading through cement. What her eyes told her brain they were seeing overrode what her brain ordered her feet to do. So, they stopped.

She felt Kit rip the fire extinguisher from her nerveless fingers. He hadn't seen it yet. Then she felt him go still beside her.

It was impossible to mistake the figure in the light from the flames. It was Puhi, or rather, the guy dressed up as Puhi, behind the shed. She had to keep telling herself it was a man in costume, because he looked different, more shark-like this time.

In the flickering yellow light, his body was sleeker, while the guy in the hangar looked like he lifted weights. Now, the mask bore sharp resemblance to a real shark's head, and she didn't see the necklace.

The chanting was a nice touch. It sounded colder and rang more hollowly than in the hangar. Kit shifted the extinguisher while she stood stock still, wondering how Puhi got that effect in the open air. And for whose benefit? If he knew they were close enough to tackle him, he didn't show it. And she wasn't about to call attention to herself.

Before Kit moved again or pulled the pin out of the extinguisher, Puhi slowly raised his arms skyward, palms up in supplication. What he did next just couldn't happen she explained to herself. Puhi walked straight into and through the burning back wall of the shed and disappeared. So did the flames.

She thought she was going to be the next one to fade away, until she got a grip on herself and on Kit's arm. He shook her off and dove for the shed, digging in his T-shirt pocket for the key.

"Give me your flashlight," he ordered.

She looked down, not realizing she'd grabbed it up along with the fire extinguisher. She ran to him and thrust it at him.

He flashed the light inside. The back wall was blackened and would need to be replaced. No one was inside the nearly empty shed.

She tried twice to get the words out before she managed it. "I expected to find him, with a headache, sitting on one of the surf boards." She heard a truck skid to a stop somewhere behind them.

"It was a trick. It had to be a trick," Kit said, stepping into the shed, muscles tensed. "There must be another way in or out or—he set it alight, saw us, and put it out somehow to impress us."

"It worked," she croaked. "I'm impressed."

Paul came panting to a halt beside her. "I sent Lono to the bulls. I came as soon as I saw flames."

"Where's Saito?" Kit asked.

Paul shrugged. "I don't know. So, who lit it?"

Kit looked at her, then Paul did, too.

"I didn't see anyone. A shadow moved then there were flames. Puhi came a minute later."

"What?" Paul's voice almost squeaked.

"And this one was different from the one in the hangar. Different build. Different costume." Kit was still staring at her. "I'm sorry, Kit. It clouded up when you went inside and I just didn't see who started it."

The moon waded out of the cloud cover at that moment to bathe them in its light, demonstrating the contrast.

"Never mind." He turned his attention to Paul. "Kimo just handed over the watch to Saito. Kimo went inside and Saito walked off toward the beach path. I went inside to go to the bathroom. Bad timing. Sorry, Paul."

Paul put his hand on Kit's shoulder. "You weren't negligent, either of you, so don't worry about it."

The two men spent the next ten minutes crawling around inside, outside, and all around the small building. The bundle of tinder was still smoking when they pulled it out. Kit stomped it into submission.

"If Saito saw someone put this here and he was watching to see who lit it, then where is he?" Kit asked Paul.

On cue, Saito came running from the direction of the beach path, reminding her of an actor who didn't know his next line. He took a good long look at the shed then at each of their faces.

"Couldn't catch him, Paul," he finally said.

"Catch who, Saito?" Paul's voice was quiet.

Saito licked his lips. "Why, the man who set the shed on fire."

"Tell us what happened." Kit flashed his light on the remains of the bundle.

Saito's eyes slid from Kit to Casey and he smiled. At least she thought he did. It was there and then it wasn't.

"I found that stuff shoved under the back of the shed yesterday, before the storm." He sounded more confidant now. "I've been keeping my eye on it. When my watch started, I told Kimo I was going to check the boats then I turned back and hid."

"Where?" Kit fired the question at him.

Saito turned and pointed. "There in the plumeria along the drive. I didn't get a good look at the guy, but I took off after him. He ran toward the beach and disappeared."

"You left the shed to burn?" Kit shot the words at him. "Why didn't you wake someone?" Casey was glad he wasn't questioning her.

Saito's voice rose with anger. "There wasn't time. I thought it was more important to try to catch the person who did it." He turned to Paul. "Look, Mr. Malo, I did what I thought was best."

"Who put out the flames, Saito?" Casey asked before she could stop herself.

For just a second the web of lies Saito was weaving sagged a little around his bewilderment. He put his hands on his hips and looked at the shed, his voice puzzled. "I don't know. It was going good." Then he caught himself. "How should I know? I was busy. I'll wet it down, just to make sure it's out."

"Good idea, Saito," Paul said. "I'll remember what you tried to do tonight for Lokelani Farms." Which might be taken two ways, Casey thought.

She stepped back as Saito moved past her toward the house. He stopped dead when he came to the fire extinguisher, laying where Kit had dropped it, its seal unbroken. She saw him clench his fists at his sides then he moved on.

Kit turned to her, his voice soft. "Did you see Saito go running off toward the beach path? I didn't."

Considering what she was seeing at the time, an elephant could have gone running off toward the beach path and she wouldn't have noticed it. But she didn't tell him that.

Instead, she answered just as softly, "He was playing it by ear. He guessed someone saw him hide the stuff under the shed, and he fitted his story around it. He thinks fairly well on his feet, that's all."

Paul, bareheaded, raked his hands through his hair. And he was barefoot. He hadn't taken time to put on his hat or boots. It's good he went to sleep with his jeans on, she thought to herself.

"If Saito is Adam's accomplice, then who are the guys taking turns playing the part of Puhi?" he asked Kit in a whisper. "And whose side are they on?"

"I don't know, Paul, but the key to all this is up there. I'll bet on it." Kit jerked his head toward the *pali*. Then he looked at her. "If Adam is leaving soon then something's going down soon. And the *pali* is where we have to go tomorrow."

Chapter 10

EVERYONE was having a late breakfast the next morning when she sleepily wandered out onto the *lanai.* She heard their voices, so she double tied her short silk kimono before she went out, her feet bare, her uncombed hair a tumble.

Coffee. She wanted it now. Kit must have seen it in her face because he had a cup ready for her by the time she got to him. She sat down at the end place at the table.

"Thanks, Kit," she whispered, wrapping both hands around the cup and slowly raising it to her lips.

It was perfect, just light enough, just sweet enough, just strong enough. Closing her eyes, she quietly smiled to herself as she sipped and savored it. She took a deep breath and gave a little shiver of delight.

She wasn't aware of the silence until she opened her eyes again. They were watching her. All of them.

James, eyes half closed, sat at the opposite end of the table with a dazed look on his face. Kimo had taken his pipe out of his mouth and was looking at her as someone would a puppy. Paul's chin rested on one hand, his intent gaze fastened on her. Even Adam's eyes held warm appreciation.

And Kit. Kit stared at her openly and open-mouthed, his expression a hybrid of fascination, wonder, and raw yearning.

She looked around their faces again, feeling warmth in her cheeks. "Good coffee," she said and reached for the toast rack.

She spread butter on a slice to the accompaniment of men clearing their throats and of chair legs scraping against the *lanai's* wooden floor boards. When she looked up again, she and Kit were alone.

"What was that all about?" she asked quietly.

"You do that every morning," he said in a stunned voice. "That little shiver. After three sips of coffee. Every morning." He gave a little shiver himself.

She was quiet for a moment. "I do? Well, you pull your left earlobe when your cup is half empty."

Kit let go of his left earlobe like it was hot. She topped off his cup from the carafe.

"You really don't have a clue, do you?" Amazement was thick in his voice. "You don't know the effect—How you look—You just reduced five adult males to slack-mouthed, gawking, adolescent idiots—"

"Will you do something for me?" she interrupted his sputterings, picking up her cup again.

"What?" he barked.

"Fix me another cup of coffee exactly the way you did this one?" She closed her eyes and sighed, taking another sip. "It's perfect."

"*Arrrgh!*" he growled, pushing himself up from the table with both hands. He stalked away, leaving her to stare after him.

She finished her coffee and toast then cleared the table, stacking everything on an inlaid wood tray. She carried it to Malama in the kitchen. Putting it on the table, she dropped into a chair and put her chin on her hand.

"Trouble, *keiki?*"

"Troubled, Malama."

Malama sat down, too, although she didn't speak. Casey looked into the depths of those knowing eyes and spilled her guts, tears burning her eyes.

"I'm scared, Malama. It's moving too fast with Kit. I can't know him the way I think I do after only a few days. I'm feeling too much. I *can't* be ready for this. Not yet."

Malama reached out and patted her arm. "Listen to your heart, Casey. Kit is a good man. There is no selfishness, no angry depths to this one. You and Kit will be okay. You wait and see." Her brown eyes danced and twinkled.

Casey smiled, hoping Malama was right, because she desperately wanted Kit to be everything he appeared to be.

She half rose and enclosed Malama in a big hug. "I forgot. You Know Things. Thanks, Malama."

By early afternoon, after bidding James good-bye and wishing him luck, they were on their way. Saito was taking James to Kauai by boat and Adam was going along for the ride. Paul gave them a lift in the truck to the trailhead. Again, as far as Adam, Saito, and Lono were concerned, they were in Ohelo at the B & B for the night.

A lightweight boogie board, shaped like a small surfboard, was strapped to each of their backpacks when they started up the trail. They poked up like sails above the backs of their heads.

"If we catch a strong wind, we might end up at the cove by the direct route. Or back at the farm, depending on the wind direction." Her lighthearted words didn't earn a decent reply.

Kit just grunted. He'd said very little to her since their strange breakfast conversation. Her stomach did flip-flops when she realized he probably felt she'd let him down last night. As a result, he was withdrawing, shutting her out, the way Luke used to do. She would gladly kick him up the trail at that moment. To keep from acting on that feeling, she simmered quietly until after they passed the waterfall.

Then she stopped, dropped her pack, and let fly. "If you have anything to say, Mr. Kahana, just say it!"

He stopped square on the trail and turned to her, a bewildered look on his face.

She plowed on. "Go ahead, yell at me. Let's clear the air. Anything to get you to stop acting like you have a burr up your—butt!"

His eyes narrowed and he stared at her. Hard. "This is your fantasy. You tell me why I should yell at you."

She was suddenly unsure of herself. "Because I let you and Paul down last night? I wasn't an asset?"

He stepped closer. "You didn't let us down, Casey. You couldn't see. I wouldn't have been able to see, either. Now, if you're over your bout of paranoia, I'll tell you about the burr I have up my butt."

She heaved a sigh of relief that he wasn't playing mind games. "You were so quiet. I thought..." If he wanted to use her for a sounding board, she'd gladly oblige. "I'm listening, boss," she ended meekly.

"Adam is leaving, right?"

"Yes, he is. He and Saito scared Kimo enough to sell out."

He shook his head. "Then why are they still trying so hard when they don't have to? Why haven't the incidents stopped?"

"Insurance because the deal isn't cut yet? Because Saito is a sadistic bastard who enjoys it? Maybe they're trying to get Paul to sell out, too?"

Now he looked worried. "He'd rather die. This half of the island has been his family's heritage since the lava cooled that formed it. I think he's safe for now because there's no survivor clause in his and Kimo's agreement. Anyway, Adam's leaving the day after tomorrow, when his shipment of macadamias is ready to go."

"Nuts to you, Adam."

He grinned. "Yeah." Then he sobered. "There's more going on here than I thought, Casey. I want to take a look at the trail to Ohelo again, just to see what I can see. If not today, then tomorrow morning. I'm going to have a look at Adam's shipment before it goes, too." He turned and walked on.

When they got close to the cave, he put his finger to his lips. "We'd better go in and take another look," he whispered.

"What if one of the Puhis is in there?" she whispered back.

Kit took off his pack and got out his flashlight, hefting it in his hand, testing its weight.

Nobody was home. Kit told her to check out her area and look for any changes since last time. When she saw the mask, necklace, and malo cloth, she was convinced it had been a different Puhi she'd seen last night.

"The food hasn't been touched," she reported.

He frowned. "Nothing is missing and nothing has been brought in. It looks like Puhi hasn't been back to stay." He moved toward the cave opening.

"Aren't you going to dance barefoot in the dirt?" she asked with a grin.

"No, this time I want him to know someone was here." He said it in a voice that gave her chills.

However, he smiled with pleasure when they got to the little beach and he saw the surf. "Like I said, good boogie board stuff. Get ready for some fun."

Kit unstrapped his board then stripped off his shorts and T-shirt. He wore his swimming briefs underneath. She sat down on a rock to enjoy the scenery.

"Watch me a while, then I'll come in and get you," he said before trotting into the waves.

"I'm all eyes, boss," she informed his retreating back.

He paddled out to the cove's mouth then turned the board toward the beach. Picking a wave, he paddled in front of it until it caught his board and carried him to shore.

She watched him until he signaled to her before he caught his next wave. By the time he got to shore, she had slipped behind a rock and put on her suit.

From where she waited, she watched him as he ran toward her. His eyelashes were dark with water, making his eyes all the bluer by contrast. His thick, dark hair rained drops of the Pacific, he needed a shave, and he was the most beautiful man she'd ever seen. And his ovely, sensuous mouth was moving.

"Are you listening, Casey?" She noted that he didn't continue ıntil she closed her mouth and nodded. "It's pretty easy, but remember hat a small wave two or three feet high has a lot of power. It can roll ⁄ou over and drag you on the bottom the whole way to shore. Let them ȝo by and catch the low ones until you have some experience."

He was patient. She was sensible. She loved it, squealing with lelight at the sensation of skimming along the surface of the water.

"You're doing great, a natural!" They waited together for a wave. 'Want to try body surfing next?"

"You have to ask?"

Soon she was riding waves without her board, planing in on her :hest and stomach. Finally, he made her stop. They rode to shore on ›ne last wave and changed behind separate rocks.

They ate the sandwiches and macadamia nut cake Malama had ;ent, then they kicked back for a while. Both of them fell asleep and he sun was sliding toward the horizon when they stirred. The sky was ι study in pinks and yellows.

Kit stood up and dug his flashlight out of his backpack. "Let's :xplore some more before it gets dark. I'd like to walk the path a little vay toward Ohelo now."

She grabbed her flashlight and followed. A stiff wind blew on the ›ther side of the *pali*. It hit them when they rounded the first turn in the ›ath. The cliffs fell away on their right toward another cove with ınother path, this one rougher. Below was a second beach that was ;eparated from their beach by a point of lava rock that jutted out into he water.

She stopped to admire the picture-postcard beach while Kit valked on, around another turn in the trail. She followed a minute or so ater.

By then she was alone. She studied the long stretch of uncleared rail, including great gaps where the cliff had fallen away. Kit wasn't ›n it. The little town of Ohelo snuggled against the foot of the *pali* in he distance to her left, on the Kauai side of the island. She noticed that ⌐okelani Farms definitely had the bigger share of the island.

She opened her mouth to call Kit's name then closed it again, ıfraid to advertise their presence. Then she was simply afraid. What if ıe'd tried to follow the trail and fallen over the edge or into one of the ȝaps? What if he'd met Puhi and lay bleeding or dead in the almost ropical vegetation that grew everywhere up here?

She backtracked around the turns on the trail to their beach path, just in case he'd found a way to somehow get behind her. Not seeing any sign of him, she went back to where she'd stood before, stopping beside a thick growth of plants that grew between two formations of lava rock.

"Kit?" she called in a soft, quavering voice, shifting her weight from one foot to the other, fighting down the panic that was rising in her.

Just as she was ready to turn and run to the farm in the fading light, the tall plants beside her parted and a hand came out, taking her by the arm.

"Casey, look—"

Her scream cut him short, echoing off the cliffs.

Kit moved quickly to cover her mouth, stifling her cry. "Get in here," he ordered impatiently.

She bit him. He jerked his hand away, shaking it and swearing while she railed at him.

"Of all the stupid things to do! First you just disappear, then you—"

Continuing to hold back the vegetation with his good hand, he yanked her through it with the bitten one. "Have hysterics later. Look what I found."

"Kahana Temps never have hysterics," she informed him coldly, turning to follow his pointing finger.

Ruins. There were two walls left standing, a stone floor, and two stone pillars that must have been the doorway once upon a time. On each pillar were petroglyphs of a big fish with big teeth. A shark.

"What is this place?" she asked, following him between the pillars.

"It's a *heiau* dedicated to a shark god."

She paused again to look around. "It sure looks different from the one behind the house."

"There's just more of it."

One minute it was dusk and the next it was dark. Kit flicked on his flashlight, its beam throwing strange shadows onto the walls. He directed the light toward the ground.

"Look at this," he said.

A perfect boot print showed in the soft ground where they hadn't stepped yet.

She bent over for a closer look. "It's a smaller foot than the one in the cave. One of our Puhis must wear boots sometimes." It paid to keep reminding herself that Puhi was just a man dressed in Puhi clothing.

She stood up and focused her light on the pillars behind them. "Do you think it's dedicated to him?"

"Puhi isn't the only shark god, and not all of them are friendly. Some *kahunas*, priests, forced the common people to build *heiaus* for them. Human sacrifices were sometimes part of the dedication ceremonies."

"How endearing," she muttered and grabbed a fistful of the back of his T-shirt as he moved away.

In places, more of the tall plants pushed up between the stones. The uneven floor, or stone platform, was difficult to walk on. Loose stones had fallen from the walls, but a path had been cleared through them. It led toward a pair of big flat stones in the floor and the two intersecting walls.

Kit flashed his light in broad sweeps back and forth in front of them. She caught a glimpse of lighter color among the dark heaps of fallen walls off to their right.

"Kit, wait." She let go of his shirt, turned on her flashlight, and swung it in that direction.

Carefully stepping from stone to stone, she was finally able to reach down and pick it up. What she held in her hand was a piece of pine board.

Kit appeared at her elbow. "It hasn't been out in the weather long. The ends are still raw looking and jagged."

She turned it over. Stamped in red on the other side was the small letter 's' and the capital letter 'M'.

"I wonder how it got up here?" she said almost to herself.

"You know what it is, don't you?" Kit asked, studying the letters. "It's part of one of the nut crates from the farm."

She sucked in her breath in recognition. "Of course. The 's' is the ending of 'Farms' and the 'M' is the beginning of 'Macadamia.'"

"Let's see what else we can find." He took her hand and towed her back to the cleared area.

The floor had sunk in one spot. Rain water and the resulting mud from the storm lay in the depression. It was too wide to jump across and too rocky to walk around it, so they walked through it. Kit still held her hand as they drew ever closer to the dark, standing walls. Finally he stopped.

He flashed his light along the wide flat stones of the floor against the back wall. "Do you see them?" he asked her.

Two sets of light brown footprints showed on the dark stones.

"Big ones and little ones, just like we're making now. They

walked through the muddy puddle, too," she observed. "That means they were here after the storm."

The smaller footprints weren't as clear, so they followed the other set until they stopped at the side wall.

"Puhi walking through walls again?" she asked in a tiny voice.

"No way. They look like they go into the wall, but they're really just beside each other. He stood here. He didn't go through the wall."

"Why would someone just stand there, facing the wall?"

He examined the wall with the light. It settled on a white scrape about waist high. "He was carrying something and rested it against the stones to get a better grip. The smaller footprints go into this little niche."

"You're good, boss," she said, and meant it.

She flashed her light along the place where the walls met, but Kit and his flashlight were there before her. He got down on his hands and knees.

"Aha!" he said and got to his feet.

"I can't believe you said that, Sherlock," she managed to say around a big grin.

"Look at this. The corner is just an optical illusion. The walls don't meet or join. The *kahunas* probably built it that way for their mysterious appearances and disappearances. Maybe they finished this part themselves. That way their secret would be safe."

"Or the workers who finished this little trick were part of the sacrifice." She looked around them nervously.

She clutched his T-shirt again as they inched single file through the space between the walls. They came out into a small room with one big slab of stone for a floor.

"Jackpot!" Kit said softly, when they saw what was inside.

Casey knelt down. "These must be the clothes that were stolen from the beach. And over there are the trail markers that were taken away."

Kit's light moved on. In a corner four crates were stacked two by two. When they stepped closer, they read 'Lokelani Farms Macadamia Nuts' stamped in red on two tops.

"Why do I think there aren't really macadamia nuts in there?" she whispered.

Kit's beam of light was on the move again. This time it found the gleam of metal in the corner beside the crates.

"A hammer and crowbar. Bring them over here." He picked up one of the top crates and carried it to the center of the room. "It's a lot ighter than the crates full of macadamia nuts at the farm." He shook it. t rattled.

She handed him the tools. "It sure sounds like macadamia nuts lacking against each other—oh!"

A stray macadamia nut on the stone floor rolled under the edge of ier boot sole, but she didn't fall. She picked it up, along with three thers she spied on the lava rock, and jammed them into her shorts ockets.

She hunkered down beside Kit. "It looks just like all the other rates in the warehouse."

"Except for this. Packing straw." Kit brushed his hand along the vhiskers of stuff sticking out between the bottom edge and the sides. We'll open it from the bottom. There's no straw showing around the op. There's probably a layer of nuts on top of whatever else is in iere." He carefully turned the crate over and picked up the crowbar.

"Easy, Kit," she warned with a gentle touch on his arm. "Don't plinter the wood."

It took a while, since the bottom was one piece. Kit pried around t several times, raising the nails out of the wood a little more each ime. With a screech and a few squeaks it finally lifted off.

A dense layer of packing straw was exposed. Kit dug his fingers nto it and lifted it up in one mass, exposing the delicate items beneath. His breath came out in a hiss, like he had a slow leak.

Casey momentarily gave up breathing. When she resumed, her vords clung to her tongue, refusing to leave without a fight.

"J-Jade. T-That's jade, Kit," she stuttered.

Chapter 11

FOUR SMALL carved jade figures nestled on the next layer of packing straw that lay over the macadamia nuts. The nuts would camouflage them if the crate was opened from the top. Casey saw two delicately carved cats, a temple dog, and one bird.

Their colors, each one different, seemed to glow in their lights. One was bright green, one bluish green, one white, and one black. She sensed just by looking at them that they would feel smooth and cool to the touch. And, when her fingers slid over them, they didn't disappoint her.

"Jade figurines." Kit looked at her expectantly, willing her to understand what they had found.

Suddenly she did and a chill came with the knowledge. "As in art theft? Honolulu? A couple of days before we got here?" Her voice was high-pitched and thin.

He nodded. "*This* is what we didn't know. *This* is why Adam and Saito want a private piece of Lokelani," he said to himself. "For now," he added grimly.

She moaned and sat down on her rear on the stone floor.

His voice went on, vibrating with excitement. "Adam brings the items to Lokelani right after the robberies, as one of the gang or the leader, or as the fence. Saito packs the stuff in crates that are shipped with all the other crates to Adam's candy factory in California. They probably come to the *heiau* by sea and use one of the beach paths. They'll have to move these crates to the warehouse in the grove soon. They've probably already taken some down."

Her words were ragged around the edges. "That's why all the stolen items have been small. Nothing can be bigger than a Lokelani macadamia nut crate."

He scowled in her direction, not really seeing her. "That will change. They're still perfecting their technique. Remember, Adam will soon have a candy factory in Europe."

"What are we going to do?" she whispered, glancing over her shoulder. She felt a presence here, a presence that watched them, assessing them and their motives.

"We're going to put this crate back together and get the hell out of here." He picked up one of the jade cats, the smallest piece, and put it in his shorts pocket.

"What are you doing?" She picked up bits of packing straw from the floor and sprinkled them into the crate.

"It's evidence of what we found here." The hammer sounded like a cannon going off each time he tapped on the nails in the bottom of the crate. "If they come for the crates tonight, we'll catch them at it."

"Define 'catch.'" There was a definite squeak in her voice.

"Not catch, exactly, more like witness them removing the crates from the *heiau*." He turned to her and made her meet his eyes. "Speaking of witnessing, listen up, Mrs. Kahana. This is important." He didn't continue until she nodded.

When he spoke in cop talk, she felt her eyes open wider with each word.

"Casey Anne Ward, you are my witness. I'm marking each of these crates with my surname initial, using my pocket knife. You have seen me remove one item from this crate, which you watched me open and then reclose."

"Oh, God," she moaned softly as he carved a tiny letter 'K' on each of the crates.

"Out. Now," he ordered as soon as he'd finished and replaced the crate and tools. He flashed his light around one last time to make sure nothing was out of place.

"What about our wet footprints?" she asked as he pulled her along the path between the fallen stones.

"We'll have to risk it." She heard the urgency in his voice and was silent after that.

He took her back to the cove, letting the moon light their way rather than his flashlight. He wouldn't let her go out onto the moonlit sand but took her into the little sandy spot behind the rocks where she had changed clothes earlier. Then he started to pace, or his version of it, in the limited space and with sand underfoot.

"If there was any way to get you out of here, I'd use it. But there isn't, so you'll have to stay with me. I don't know which way they're coming, or if they're coming tonight, although they're together out on the water already."

She'd forgotten about Saito and Adam taking James to Kauai by boat that afternoon.

"What's your plan?" she asked quietly, pouring him a cup of coffee from the new thermos Malama had sent. Its shiny stainless steel cup glinted in the moonlight.

He stopped in front of her and took the cup she offered. "Hide our stuff here. Watch the cave, watch the *heiau*. Try to find out who Puhi is and his connection to these two. I can't be two places at once, though."

It took only a second for her to make her decision. "I can watch the cave, this beach path, and the farm side of the *pali* trail, if you'll take the *heiau* and the second beach path."

He swore then gave her a long, measuring look before he spoke again. "Don't forget your hat. Your hair almost glows in the moonlight and starlight," he said softly.

He put down his coffee and took her by the shoulders, lifting her to her feet. His voice was rough. "Promise me you won't take any chances? Don't go inside the cave for any reason. Remember, we're only watching. There's an even chance they won't come until tomorrow night. By that time I can have the state police here."

"I promise," she answered softly. Before she realized what she was about to do, she threw her arms around his neck. Her words came out muffled against his T-shirt, her voice fierce. "Be careful, Kit, and don't do anything stupid. You're such a big target."

His arms pulled her closer. "That's what the guys on the force used to tell me."

She pushed herself away from him and looked up into his eyes. "Don't go back to it, Kit. Please? Learn to type and come to work for Kahana Temps. Or, with that cute little Hawaiian butt, you could be a male model. Any job that doesn't involve high-speed chases, bullets, blunt instruments, switchblades, or people from Psychotics R Us."

He grinned down at her. "There might be another job in the works. But right now I wish you'd just shut up and kiss me, Casey Kahana." His voice was husky and deep and slid along her nerve endings like the words of an old Hawaiian love song. "Do I have to do everything around here?" he added.

If the kiss that followed didn't prove to him that she could pull her own weight in that department, it wouldn't be for lack of trying. She was pleased when he had to sit down before they climbed the beach path again.

Without the aid of flashlights, they found a small, oval-shaped area at the edge of the trail, a short distance away from where they watched the cave last time. It was more protected than the other area, screened by plants and the lava rock itself. Kit left the thermos with her, saying he would be able to stay awake better without caffeine than she would. He helped her bend down half the plants that blocked her view of the cave area, then he reluctantly left her there, sitting on her mat and blanket.

She watched until he disappeared around the first turn in the path, hating the thought of him spending the night anywhere near the ancient Hawaiian *heiau* where modern-day, heavy-duty crooks had hidden their loot. It bothered her more that those same crooks were expected to remove said loot any minute now. She prayed Kit would keep his head and simply observe rather than act. Knowing that she couldn't have stopped him if she tried was little comfort.

She scarcely had time to get a good worry going before Puhi came home, almost at a run, by way of the *pali* trail from the farm. The man, wearing dark shorts and a T-shirt, slipped between the rock and the *pali* to go into the cave. Would he come out nearly naked and wearing that horrible mask?

She relaxed a little when he reappeared, still clothed, on top of the rock where he set up the short-wave radio and made a transmission. She strained to hear what he said but wasn't able to make out the hushed words. When he finished, he left the radio where it was, which was more frightening, and hurried past her, toward the *heiau*.

Her breathing stopped all on its own; she couldn't have moved if her life depended on it. Her nose and her eyes, however, still worked. He passed so close to her hiding place that she caught the clean-clothes smell of him. He was Hawaiian, well-muscled, and, she would bet, the Puhi from the hangar. And she had never seen his face before.

She sat another tense half hour or so, ears straining for any sounds other than those of nature, before she concentrated on relaxing her tight muscles. That was a mistake, because it wasn't long before she felt herself grow sleepy. Reaching for the thermos of coffee, she poured herself a cupful. The stainless steel cup caught the moonlight, so she wrapped the edge of her blanket around it.

The sea behind and below her and the wind in the leaves all around her teamed up for a duet on a lullaby, while the moon began flirting with the clouds, winking and dodging.

She was drifting, not asleep, not fully awake, when someone slapped a wide, sticky piece of tape firmly over her mouth. A split second later her hat was knocked off and a rough, prickly sack came down over her head, while her hands were caught in a coarse rope that tightened to make them useless when she tried to flail at her attackers.

She sensed there were two of them but they didn't speak, maintaining an uncanny silence between them. The only sounds came from her. She recognized two things, though, that verified for her who they were: Adam's cologne and the feel of cold carved metal in the small of her back, a tiki belt buckle. So, she and Kit were right. Big Footprints and Little Footprints were Saito and Adam.

Saito's hands were busy on her body. Her boot connected with his shin and she heard a satisfying yelp of pain. Then she felt a gentle hand, which had to be Adam, snake up under the burlap sack that cocooned her head. He applied pressure on the side of her neck, then everything went quiet and black.

SHE CAME TO her senses, bound hand and foot and slung over someone's shoulder. Saito's? She was being carried through a narrow rocky place, and she forced herself to remain limp despite the many parts of her body that came into contact numerous times with the lava rock.

Saito put her down none to gently on her side against a wall. Someone cushioned her head when it would have smacked painfully against the stone floor. Adam again? The macadamia nuts in her pocket felt like boulders beneath her left hip.

She continued her unconscious act, praying Adam wouldn't leave her alone with Saito for a moment. Strong light filtered through the burlap but the shadows were indistinct. When she heard the scrape of wood on stone, she guessed they were picking up the crates and that she was in the small room of the *heiau*. Then it was dark and she knew they had gone.

A new dread ripped through her. Where was Kit and what had they done to him that he hadn't helped her? Was he unconscious, or worse, close to her there in the darkness or outside on the trail? And where was the guy who played Puhi?

She struggled against her bonds in a frenzy of fear. Saito had tied her hands behind her back too tightly...and enjoyed every minute of it, she bet. Her fingers were numb, but not so numb that she didn't feel the fingernail she bent back as she tried to work some slack into the chafing rope. She managed to get the fingernail going the right way again.

Tears of frustration and unrelenting fear poured down her face to wet the burlap. The tape across her mouth seemed a less painful project to work on while she rested. Trying to loosen it, she pushed at it with ıer tongue and worked her jaws.

It was then that a whisper of sound and a steady light told her she vasn't alone any longer. She lay perfectly still, sure that whoever was here would see and hear her heart trying to get out of her chest. The ears stopped, she was too terrified to cry.

She prayed it wasn't Saito coming back to do heaven knew what o her, and possibly to Kit, in revenge for that kick in the shins and all he other resentments he'd built up against her in his tiny, criminal nind.

Then Kit's dear voice started saying dreadful things in Hawaiian ınd English, with a little Portuguese thrown in for good measure.

She distinctly heard her name in the murky torrent of appalling vords. "*Mumph-m-m*," she answered and moved.

He ended his litany of curses with a sound, halfway between a ob and a sigh. With great care he lifted her to a sitting position against he wall...then seemed to lose control. He ripped the sack off her head, iving her a heavy brush burn on her cheek. She forgot her burning heek, however, when he tore the tape off her mouth. She fully xpected to see her lips stuck to it.

He begged her to speak to him, so she did. "The fine hairs on my ace will probably grow back as a full beard after that, Kit! I'll have to oin a carnival side show."

Meanwhile, he was sawing on the ropes at her wrists with his ocket knife. She wondered if she was bleeding yet. Maybe she wasn't ıble to feel the cuts because her hands were so numb. As soon as they vere free, she counted her nerveless fingers then checked her lips. All vere present and accounted for as she wiped her mouth on the hem of ıer tank top.

As soon as Kit freed her feet, he grabbed her arms and pulled her ıpright, bringing on a wave of nausea and dizziness. He supported her ıgainst his body when her knees buckled. She thought she was used to ain by that time, but she groaned when pins and needles, more like arge thorns and knitting needles, started stabbing through her blood-tarved extremities.

"A man came back to the cave—" she began.

"It was Mike Akoa, Malama's son," he interrupted. "He wouldn't et me help you until Adam and Saito had gone. He went after them. His men are waiting all along the beach paths. Stomp your feet and hake your hands!" Before she did either he pulled her to him in a hug hat now put her ribs in danger.

She wrapped her useless arms around his waist and held on as tightly as she could manage, reveling in his presence and the safety of his arms.

"I'm okay, Kit, really. I think my thermos cup shining in the moonlight is what gave me away to them. And I'm certain Adam kept Saito from doing as much damage as he wanted to do."

"How do you know that?" He pulled back to look at her.

"Trust me, his touch was a lot less personal than Saito's, and gentler. Saito would have belted me to knock me out. Adam pressed on the side of my neck." She gingerly slid her hand along her jawbone and down her neck. Her head was starting to throb in time with her heartbeat.

Light from Kit's flashlight bathed the little room. He relaxed his grip and took the hand she'd raised. He turned it over and brought her wrist to his lips, gently kissing the red, raw lines on her skin made by the ropes. Her knees threatened to buckle again, for a different reason this time.

"Saito did this to you?" he asked quietly, first raising both her wrists to the light then lightly touching the raw, weeping places on her upper arms where she'd brushed the lava rock.

She gasped at what she saw in his eyes and face. She touched his cheek tenderly. "Don't look like that, Kit, please. Calm down. Mike will get him."

The awful mask slipped and her Kit smiled down at her. "Let's get out of here. I want to hear all the details from Mike." He supported her with one arm and carried the flashlight in his other hand.

But a complication developed in that plan when they came face to face with Saito outside on one of the wide, flat stones in the *heiau* floor.

The clouds were gone and the place was glowing with moonlight, giving it an awful beauty. Saito's eyes moved from Kit to her then back again. Kit let go of her, put down his flashlight, and took a few steps forward, putting himself between her and Saito. She shifted her position to peek around Kit and see what was happening.

"You're under arrest, Saito," Kit said in a voice that almost made her reach for the sky.

Saito shot her a venomous look. "Is she a cop, too?"

"No, she isn't a cop. We can do this the easy way or the hard way. Your choice."

Kit's tone let her know that he wanted a piece of Saito. The two men eyed each other across four feet of space.

"Let's do it the hard way, cop. After I take you out, your

girlfriend's leaving with me. Gonna have some fun with her."

Kit growled deep in his throat as, obeying a silent signal, both of them assumed martial arts stances, knees and elbows bent, hands open. Saito's cold smile told her he was confident that he had the advantage in the confined space, being smaller and more wiry. And not being blindingly angry.

As she watched them slowly circle each other, her fists pressed against her sides and a new pain joined the others. The macadamia nuts in her pockets were pressing against her many bruises.

It would take just one of them underfoot. Experience had taught her that. She aimed, working against dizziness, her pounding head, and a gut-wrenching fear. Saying a silent prayer, she rolled all four of the smooth brown rock-hard nuts in a tight pattern onto the flat stone where Saito had stopped. She studied his face in profile and sensed that he was ready to attack.

Remembering what Paul had said about covering all the bases, she added a fervent prayer to Puhi, asking that he protect Kit from his own anger and from the man who meant to hurt them.

At that moment a sound filled the *heiau*. Both men slowly stood upright and looked around. Chanting. It started as gently as a soft breeze then grew into a gale force wind. It came from above them and below them and from the ancient stones themselves, its chilling echoes surrounding them. She heard herself whimper and her eyes flew to Kit's, seeking reassurance there.

Suddenly Saito's face twisted with fear. He swayed and took one step back. The macadamia nuts made a chattering sound as they rolled beneath his cowboy boots on the lava rock. His feet shot out from under him and, with a sickening thud that she felt through her feet, he went down. And was still. The chanting stopped.

"And your mama, too," she said unevenly to Saito's motionless form.

She watched, not breathing, when Kit moved forward to stand over Saito, his fists clenching and unclenching at his sides. Then he looked at her.

In that moment she listened to what her heart was telling her about Christopher Allan Kahana, and she let it speak silently for her through her eyes. She hoped they were filled to overflowing with the love she felt for him, willing him to think of her and not the helpless man at his feet, a man who would have nothing to do with them after this night.

Before either of them moved, a figure came bursting through the bushes, between the pillars, and onto the stone platform, gun drawn. Casey had a moment of terror before she recognized him as the man from the cave, Mike Akoa. Since she'd last seen him, he had acquired an egg-sized lump on the left side of his forehead.

He looked down at Saito with a satisfied smile. "The one that got away. Good work, Chris." He pulled shiny handcuffs out of the waistband of his shorts.

He rolled Saito over, bringing his limp hands behind his back. "Aloha," he said, looking up at her with a big grin. "You're the Amazon from the hangar. Gonna take on a shark god with nothing but a honkin' big wrench and a colorful vocabulary." He shook his head good-naturedly, glancing from one to the other.

Kit still silently stared at her. The answering emotion she saw in his eyes made her lightheadedness worse. Her neck ached where Adam had done whatever he'd done and suddenly she couldn't see Kit clearly.

She seemed to be floating off her feet as the moonlight faded from silver to dull gray. Her name echoed off the walls while she watched Kit perform an amazing feat. In slow motion he gracefully leaped over the prone Saito and the kneeling Mike to catch her in his arms before she hit the stones. Then came darkness.

SHE CAME to as a medic from Mike's team was examining her. He put an ice pack on her neck and told her she would have to sleep off the effects of Adam's knockout pressure point.

Then Kit carried her down to their beach to a police launch. He put her down gently on a bunk in the cabin and sat on the bunk's edge while the launch brought them to the Lokelani Farms dock where Paul met them in the Jeep. At the house, Malama greeted them at the door and made each of them drink a cup of herbal tea. Only then was Casey allowed to clean herself up.

The time she was in the shower was the only time she was out of Kit's sight, and then he insisted that Malama stay with her. When they came out of the bathroom, he was pacing the floor on his side of the open connecting door. She and Malama sat down on her bed with witch hazel and an antibiotic ointment in hand.

At first he watched silently from the doorway. Then, when she winced or sucked in her breath at Malama's tender ministrations, he'd do a turn or two around his room, muttering darkly in Hawaiian. Malama finally spoke to him in Hawaiian and closed the door while she tended to the bruises and scrapes that didn't show, under the silk kimono. Casey dressed herself in jeans and a long-sleeved T-shirt after Malama finished.

Now, Kit watched every move she made from across the kitchen table where they sat with Malama, Mike, Paul, Kimo, and Lono. She insisted on hearing the details before she went to her bed.

Adam and Saito were in custody. The stolen jade from the crates in the *heiau* and in the warehouse in the grove, including the cat Kit had put in his pocket, had been recovered.

"Adam had big plans for Lokelani Farms." Mike held an ice pack on his forehead. "We think he and Saito used it to move items from the first three robberies. We picked up on Adam after the third one. With him staying in the cottage, he and Saito could meet any time they liked, and they had easy access to the boats. The farm passed Adam's test runs, so he set out to buy Kimo's share. The new candy factory in Europe would have made it easier for them to internationally distribute the stolen items through the candy shipments."

Paul took a moment to fill in Mike on what had been going on around the farm. Mike said that Saito probably carried out the pranks he and Adam thought up. And he was sure Saito never saw him or anything 'not human' on or near the *pali*.

Mike agreed that James's interference had been a bonus to Adam and Saito, throwing in red herrings and muddying the waters. He also agreed with Kit about the moved trail markers being a cover-up prank for Adam.

Mike glanced at Kimo. "Adam and Saito both volunteered that you didn't know anything about their activities, so you're in the clear. Saito's giving us everything we want to know, but he's making us work for it. Eventually, he'll tell us everything about Adam's art theft ring for a reduced sentence."

Kimo appeared more relaxed than Casey had ever seen him. "Adam and I were at school together. He knew all about my superstitions and used them against me. I should have listened to you, Paul."

Mike looked at Paul, his expression grim. "You would have been in real danger after Adam owned part of the farm. I think that's why the pranks didn't stop, even after Kimo agreed to sell. I'm sure you would have had a fatal accident very shortly after you signed the new partnership papers."

Malama's breath came out in a hiss at her son's words.

Paul calmly took a sip of his coffee. "You're probably right. Adam was insisting on an iron-clad survivor clause in any partnership arrangement we made. If I died, he would have owned everything."

Casey shuddered at the thought of what would have happened here if Adam and Saito hadn't been stopped. "You were the one who stayed in the cave, Mike?" she asked, taking a small sip of her tea. She had seen Malama pour a liquid into this cupful.

Malama finally spoke. "My Michael climbed all over the *pali* when he was a *keiki*."

Mike smiled and nodded. "I was picked for this task force stakeout because I knew the island and because I have excellent night vision. My men bought supplies for me on Kauai and dropped off whatever I needed on the second beach, the rough one. They were offshore, pretending to be fishermen. I cleared just enough of the trail on the farm side to make it easier to get up and down to Lokelani Farms."

He grinned at his mother. "I kept my old Puhi costume in the cave. When I recognized Kit, I decided to wear it so he wouldn't recognize me."

"When Casey described Puhi to me," Malama told her son, "I knew it was your Puhi costume that you wore in the Aloha Week parade years ago. I was very worried, but I couldn't reach you. All I could do was wait."

"Sorry, Mom." Mike put his arm around Malama's shoulders.

"The sound effects were spectacular in the hangar." Kit's eyes glinted.

Mike laughed. "Sorry about that hard fall, Chris. You know how to land better than that. I was searching Adam's plane that night. It was a long shot but I decided to try to scare you off. I hid in an old storage bin and got out of the hangar through another door at the back."

"Did you take the ring boxes out of Kit's plane?" Casey asked him.

"No, it must have been Saito."

She shivered. Kit stirred in his chair, his face darkening.

At the time Mike was in the hangar, he didn't know about the pranks, but he said he realized that something else must be going on and that Paul brought in Kit to help him out.

"You and Casey were everywhere and I realized it wouldn't take you long to figure it out, maybe put yourselves in danger. But the higher-ups wouldn't let me fill you in."

Mike gave his mother a squeeze and continued. "The cave was perfect for a base camp. Saito and Adam didn't know about it, but I knew about the *heiau*. When I checked it out a few months ago, I found empty crates, packing straw, and burlap sacks full of macadamia nuts in the hidden room. When the fourth robbery went down, we were ready. Next time I checked, the crates weren't empty anymore."

Mike put down the ice pack and continued. "I had to go to Honolulu to report. When I got back tonight, I came to the house to tell you guys what was going on and to get Mom and Paul to confirm in the guest book the dates of Adam's visits to the farm. They were always a day or so after the dates of the robberies."

Mike told them he misjudged the number of crates in the warehouse before it was locked. He realized it when Paul told him earlier that night that the shipment was going out in a few days. He knew Adam and Saito would have to make their move soon, maybe that same night, since his men reported that the two were on Kauai anyway.

Mike shook his head in disbelief. "Then Mom and Paul told me where you two were. Paul's radio suddenly wouldn't send out of this valley no matter what I did. I've never climbed that *pali* path so fast in my life. I stopped at the cave just long enough to radio my men to move in closer, land men on each beach path, and wait for my signal."

Casey spoke up. "I watched you do it. I was sitting right there and you didn't see me."

"It would have been better for you if I had." Regret weighted the words. "When Adam and Saito spied you, they didn't know what to do. They couldn't get past without you seeing them. And if you saw them, the operation they'd worked so hard for here would be lost. Adam didn't want to hurt you, but they decided to take you as a bargaining point in case they ran into Kit, who had to be around somewhere. Why they just didn't come back here and wait until tomorrow night is beyond me."

Casey's and Kit's eyes caught and held. They understood why. Saito pushed for taking her because he wanted to get his hands on her. He would have somehow come back for her, even if everything had gone smoothly. And she knew in her heart that Kit would not have been allowed to live if Saito had come across him.

According to Saito, Mike said, Adam insisted they be silent so she wouldn't know who they were. They didn't think Kit and Casey had figured out their operation, that Casey was just watching for someone coming over the *pali* to do mischief on the farm. Adam and Saito didn't know they had found the *heiau* or that Mike and his team were onto them.

"Anyway," Mike continued, "Kit confronted me on the trail after

I made my radio call. He recognized me and we were coming back for you, Casey, when I got the signal, by way of a vibrating pager, that Adam and Saito were on their way to the beach. We went inside the *heiau* and took cover behind a heap of stones from a fallen wall hoping you would be okay where you were. When Saito carried you in I had to use all my training, and then some, to quietly restrain Kit."

She looked from Mike to Kit and back again, amazed that Mike had been able to do so.

Mike caught her look and added with a grin, "I know some disabling tactics myself. We saw you move and heard you make a noise, so we knew you were alive. He went to you as soon as I would let him, after Adam and Saito carried out the four crates and left the *heiau*."

"And Saito somehow got past you," Kit said quietly.

Mike grimaced at the gentle rebuke. "He was a little distance behind Adam on the path and one of my men dislodged a rock. He dropped the crates he carried and took off. When he got to the top of the path, at the same time I did, he knocked me stupid with one punch to the head; his fists are like iron. He was heading back to the *heiau* for Casey because he knew it was over. Saito carried a switchblade and he had a gun hidden in the *heiau* room. It would have been a hostage situation. But you had everything well in hand by the time I got there."

Kit shook his head. "Your chanting is what threw Saito off guard," he said. "That's why he stepped on those macadamia nuts Casey rolled out behind him. I didn't do anything, though I wanted to feel my hands around his throat."

"That chant made my hair stand on end." Casey shivered again.

Mike shook his head and his face wore a puzzled look. "I didn't chant tonight. The only time I chanted was in the hangar. It gave me the creeps and I didn't do it again."

Casey looked at Kit. "But-but someone chanted tonight in the *heiau*," she stuttered. "And the Puhi who put out the fire in the storage shed chanted, too. Was that one of your men?"

Mike slowly shook his head. "I worked alone the whole time. I kept in touch with my men on the boat by radio. Like I said, I just got back from Honolulu tonight. Was there a fire?" He looked from them to his mother.

"Remember, *keikis*," Malama said softly, "there are many things beyond explanation in Hawaii. You can believe what you like, but I believe what you saw and heard both those times was our *aumakua*, Puhi, fulfilling his promise to protect Lokelani and those who love it.

"'This corner of the earth smiles for me beyond all others,'" she quoted, looking past him to watch the waves roll in. "Horace, no less. I wondered if I'd ever find that place and now I have. But I have to get back to Honolulu," she ended soberly, meeting his eyes. Whatever they had between them or were about to have between them, the real world still called.

His eyes twinkled like blue devils danced behind them. "You have to stay here until those bruises fade. What would Aunt Patty say? Besides, Paul and I had another long talk last night. He's invited us to stay for the rest of the two weeks he booked us for. His treat."

"Paul is such a sweetie." And she grinned at the thought of Patty Kahana's face if she heard half of what had gone on here. But her smile faded because her heart was heavy. "I can't believe our adventure here is over, Kit."

He squeezed her hands. "Maybe it isn't. Do you remember my telling you about my uncle on the Big Island, about spending my summers working on his ranch? Well, Paul wants me to be the new foreman of Lokelani Farms."

Her smile was wide with relief and delight at the excitement in his face and voice. "That's great, Kit. I'm glad you're not going back to police work."

His words suddenly took on a careful note. "That's not all. Kimo still wants to sell out. I have quite a bit of money saved and invested, so I'm buying a share of Lokelani Farms. Paul is buying out the rest of Kimo's share. I'll be a part owner, a small part, as well as the foreman. That means a percentage plus a salary."

She squealed with delight and hugged him. "I'm so happy for you." She tried to turn away so he wouldn't see the tears in her eyes.

He wouldn't let her go, dropping a soft kiss on her shoulder. "Paul's offered you a salaried job, too. He wants you to computerize Lokelani's records and operations and help him in the office with reservations and stuff. And Malama has some ideas she wants to bounce off you, too, about her teas and liniments."

"I'd like that, Kit. This is a great place to work."

"This is a great place for a lot of things, Mrs. Kahana." Tenderness softened the words he spoke then. "Casey, the deed to the cottage is part of the deal I made with Paul...in case you say yes when I ask you to marry me."

She gasped and her amazed gaze flew to his face as he continued. He looked like a worried little boy, uncertain and vulnerable.

"Will you marry me, Casey? I love you to distraction. If you don't, I won't be any good to Paul or anyone else."

She finally managed to get the words out around the wonder and joy that surged through her like a storm tide. "We've only known each other a few days, Kit. How can we be in love like this?"

"You, too, huh?"

"Me, too, boss, but I was afraid to believe it."

"Well, believe it. And apparently, a few days is long enough for us." He smiled gently. "Listen to your heart."

"You've been talking to Malama," she accused, laughing and crying at the same time.

"Guilty." He was suddenly serious again. "And my heart tells me I want to spend the rest of my life watching you wake up in the mornings and bringing you Kona coffee so I can see that little shiver you do. What do you say?"

He grinned and his dimples beckoned. Before he moved, she did what she'd been wanting to do ever since she'd first seen them. She drilled into both of them with her index fingers. "I hope all our babies have dimples like their father."

"That's a yes?" he asked, capturing her hands again and bringing her fingertips to his lips.

"You bet it is," she replied, amazement in her voice. Then she grinned up at him mischievously. "Not many couples are married before they're engaged. I promise that you're in for the loving of your life, Mr. Kahana."

In answer he reached up and tugged on his left earlobe, a gentle smile on his face.

She pulled back in puzzlement. "There's not a coffee cup in sight, half empty or otherwise."

"It's my loving cup that's empty, Mrs. Kahana, and only you can fill it to brimming." He pulled her closer against him.

They stood quietly in each other's arms, listening to the sounds of home and to the most ancient chants of all—the sea sighing against the shore, the wind whispering in the casuarina trees...and two hearts beating as one.

~ * ~

Sharon K. Garner

Sharon enjoys writing stories about love and danger set in exotic locations. A former library cataloguer and newspaper proofreader, she keeps her hand in with freelance proofreading/light copy editing. She lives with her welder/EMT husband of many years, a man who no longer flinches when asked such questions as, “How long does it take to bleed to death?” and, “How can I disable a big piece of equipment?” Two demanding cats with opposite personalities complete the household. In her free time, the author reads English mysteries and regularly prances around the living room doing walk aerobics, all the while keeping an appreciative eye on her small collection of Tiffany-style lamps and her significantly larger collection of crystal figurines. Visit her at http://www.sharonkgarner.com.

Printed in the United Kingdom by
Lightning Source UK Ltd., Milton Keynes
142215UK00001B/7/A